SLEEPERS

Delena Epstein

Contents

Dedication

To all my fellow insomniacs,
who like to read by the light of the moon!

"Apocalypse is a frame of mind." [Nicodemus] said then. "A belief. A surrender to inevitability. It is a despair for the future. It is the death of hope."

—Jim Butcher, Death Masks

Chapter 1

"GOOD morning, Boston. This is Daniel Decker from CBS Boston, the SkyEye for your early news and traffic reports. It is a beautiful Thursday and it seems spring is coming early this year. There isn't a cloud in the sky and after our long and difficult winter, I'm pleased to let you know that we have a temperature of 62F, and today we will reach a high of sixty-five by midafternoon. Let's hope the weather holds out for a sunny weekend."

"Interstate 90 and Interstate 93 traffic is flowing nicely . . .

"Wait . . . what the hell! I can't believe what I'm seeing. Suddenly, there's a thirty-to-forty-car pileup where Interstate 90 and Interstate 93 converge into Boston. Traffic is grinding to a standstill and people are getting out of their cars. Astonishing! What . . .? People are crumpling to the ground . . . those still standing are leaning over to help, but no one is getting back up. Wait . . . there's another one on Highway 1. Traffic appeared to be traveling at a leisurely rate—I can't understand why the large pileups!"

". . . Dan, excuse the interruption . . . we have breaking news. This is Savannah Atwood at CBS headquarters. This anomaly appears to have first taken place in Boston, but is beginning to manifest in California, Utah, and Florida, so far. We are monitoring news reports from European Union and Switzerland. It appears that at approximately 7:01 a.m., the same phenomena may have begun worldwide. People are collapsing by the thousands.

"We have just received word the FFA has canceled all domestic and international flights. They are rerouting all flights in midair to the nearest airports. Dan, if Logan air traffic control has not already contacted your helicopter pilot, please tell him to land immediately."

"Roger that. We're looking for the closest location to land, but our listeners should note that I see dozens of emergency vehicles and police vehicles headed towards the interstate. I don't see any more people collapsing, and those still standing appear to be doing their best to assist those lying on the ground."

Savannah cleared her throat and took a deep breath before continuing. "This could be a bioterrorist attack. Law enforcement and Homeland Security officials are advising all citizens to remain in your homes. If you are driving, please stop, pull your car to the side of the road, and walk to avoid further accidents. The President has banned all public transportation for the immediate future. For parents with school-age children, tune in to KPBC. Each school district will relate instructions for the orderly release of students. For working parents and caretakers unable to reach the schools, you need not worry, as all suitable public schools will act as emergency shelters until this incident is resolved. The Red Cross is mobilizing and supervising the transition of public buildings to shelters at this time, and we will broadcast information as we receive it."

"Savannah, we've just landed in a field close to Interstate 93 and we are going to determine what's happening," Dan said his voice raw and breathless as he began to run toward the highway.

"Our cameraman, Edward Louis is with me and we will be showing live feed as soon as possible."

"Dan, this is Savannah once again. Reports are coming in of a subway train crash at the 43rd street station and two airplanes have reportedly gone down near Logan International. We have no numbers of injured or fatalities at this time. We will stay with you as long as we can . . . Oh my God, it's now 8:01, and reports are coming in from dozens of states about people collapsing. My co-anchor Josh Bradford has just collapsed next to me. Our producer has assured me that Josh has a pulse and they are making him comfortable on the floor as we speak. What is happening? . . . My God, one of our cameramen has just fallen . . .

"A statement has just been issued by the White House. President Mitchell has activated all National Guard units and there is a six o'clock curfew nationwide. Looting has already begun in some cities here and abroad. Mass hysteria is emerging in some places as government officials and scientists frantically try to determine the cause. If this is a deadly virus, and if it is, who is responsible? Hospitals in some areas have announced they are at maximum capacity and the military and National Guard are arranging to house victims in tents and the government is requesting all doctors and nurses to volunteer to care for the victims."

"Savannah, Dan here. I have with me a witness to the local situation. James Jackson, of Boston. Can you tell us what you saw this morning?"

The man turned to the camera, his face drawn tight with fear. "Morning traffic was flowing easily when suddenly the car in front of me slowed down and gradually came to a stop. I figured the car must have died and the minute I got out of my car to see if I could help the driver out, that's when the lady behind me rear-ended me. From that point on it was like bumper cars at a carnival. Maybe thirty cars involved. I don't think anyone was hurt too badly because traffic was slow—"

"What happened to the other driver?" Dan shifted the mic from Jackson to himself and back again in a single fluid motion.

"—anyway, when I checked the driver, he was slouched over his steering wheel. When I opened his car door, he fell to the side and landed on the ground. He was still breathing, but I couldn't wake him up. Other people got out of their cars too and then a lot of them just fell to the ground." James said. The longer he talked, the louder his voice became. "This has to be an attack by ISIS, North Korea, or Iran. They finally found a way to terrorize the United States. I have to get to my wife; she's not answering her cell phone."

Dan reached out and wrapped his arm around James and squeezed, then turned back to his mic. "Savannah, you heard it here first. As I walked down the road, I saw people passed out in their cars and lying on the pavement and in the grass on the highway shoulders. If this is a viral pandemic, it works fast. Are there any reports from public health departments yet about how we should protect ourselves? The positive in this situation is that people appear to be sleeping or in a coma. I haven't seen any blood or wounds of any kind, and despite the car crashes, no one is reporting any serious injuries in this vicinity. Back to you, Savannah."

"The President of the United States will address the nation shortly. Homeland Security has promised an hourly bulletin on all developments. Hopefully it won't be long before we have some answers for the American people."

Chapter 2

THE James S. Brady Press Briefing Room at the White House was abnormally quiet as reporters waited for the President of the United States to appear for his speech. Normally there was joking amongst themselves and gossiping about agenda items for that day. Today, however, everyone spoke in hushed whispers.

In a joint effort between the media networks and satellite television companies, the military prearranged the time slot so the government could take control of all major networks, placing the President's speech on multiple channels. Homeland Security, working with other nations arranged for a simultaneous broadcast in the European Union, Canada, France, and a handful of other countries.

The picture of the president' podium switched to Savannah Atwood from CBS news. In her early thirties, her blonde hair flared just past her chin in a style that framed her face. Her bright blue eyes and her serious expression made people, lean forward, even in their living rooms, to listen to her hushed voice as she spoke.

"President Mitchell is due within the next five minutes to address the people of the United States. Kenneth Mathews, his press secretary, announced a few minutes ago that the president would not be answering questions following his speech. Rumors are circulating among the press that Vice President Baker was a victim of yesterday's occurrence. Occurrence is the term everyone is using as we are still in the dark about what happened to the millions of people who collapsed and have yet to awake. Tension around the world is high, as you would expect, and despite the request from the White House yesterday about avoiding wild speculation, that is exactly what media across the country have done. We've heard theories about bioterrorists, aliens, global warming, and we have even heard speculation that this is the beginning of the Biblical apocalypse. CBS has refrained from wild speculations although we have discussed it being a terrorist attack, but we've reported only on information the White House has released. Our reporters on the streets have observed that looting has increased in various areas of Boston and that someone set fire to a strip mall near Boston University. Firefighters assisted by the National Guard quickly quelled the blaze . . ." Atwood suddenly stopped and touched her earpiece. "Wait . . . the president is entering the briefing room."

The camera switched back to the podium and President Mitchell nodded as the press corps took their seats. Normally when the POTUS appeared the press applauded, but this day was unlike any other in the history of mankind and the press remained respectful and subdued.

"My fellow Americans, after the events that took place worldwide yesterday, I am as devastated, as I know you are. We have all suffered personally. My daughter and the Vice President both collapsed yesterday, and my heart bleeds for all the families of those affected.

"I come before you today to share what information we have about the occurrence, as this event is popularly called, and to assure you that we are doing everything within our power to help victims and assist their families. I have been in touch with most world leaders, including

Iran and China—their countries have experienced the same tragedy as the United States and their scientists have joined our in searching for answers."

The President paused for a brief moment, his anguish clearly visible on his face. "Yesterday morning at precisely 7:01 a.m. people began to mysteriously collapse in Boston. This phenomenon continued every hour on the hour at various points in the United States and around the world until 12:01 a.m. There have been no incidents since then. Our initial reports estimate that 11 percent of the US population are victims of this occurrence. That is approximately thirty-five million people in the United States alone."

Reporters in the room gasped and the President waited until the room quieted once again. "In addition to the collapses yesterday, there were also two plane crashes and a subway collision. The death toll is 894. Local government agencies are withholding the names of the victims until we can notify family members. As you know, there were a great number of vehicular accidents on the nation's streets and highways, and we are still receiving and compiling data on injuries and fatalities."

The President bowed his head for a brief moment as if in prayer before continuing. "Early this morning I petitioned Congress and was granted an executive order to deal with this catastrophe. We have developed an initial plan to render aid to those affected, and to determine the cause. One of our first priorities is to stop civil unrest. Looters will be arrested and face harsh penalties. We are declaring martial law and a six o'clock curfew in all time zones is in effect for the immediate future. Secondly, all businesses not connected with essential services are to remain closed for the next seventy-two hours. Wall Street and banks will remain closed as well to reduce massive panic and avoid a rush to empty accounts or sell stocks off. We have closed our borders and halted public transportation until we have further answers. We have raised our threat assessment to Imminent. Since threat assessments normally address terrorism, we have reverted to the color system. Red is the highest threat assessment and is severe. Therefore, we are Imminent Red.

"I will now introduce you to some officials and explain what their functions are. They will stand when I call their names and they will each hold a separate press conference scheduled within the next few days to give you updates and answer your questions. We will be as transparent as possible, hopefully giving the American people faith that their government is doing all that it can. As soon as we have verifiable information, we will issue a press release. I am asking the press to avoid wild speculation so that it does not frighten the American people any further.

"Since the Vice President is incapacitated, Supreme Court Justice Wellman swore Senator Jared Smith from Texas into office as Vice President Pro Tempore at 3:00 a.m. this morning.

"General Corbin Harrison is in charge of all military operations and is assigning an officer to each state to oversee military personnel and all medical facilities. For lack of a better term, we are calling these facilities tent cities. Military personnel are constructing them and twenty-five of them are already operable. Each holds five hundred bunk beds, stacked two high. Within the next week, it is our goal to have a bed for everyone. US companies now have contracts for both wooden and metal bunk beds as well as EKG machines and other necessary medical equipment and supplies. These companies will need workers and the information about where to apply will be broadcast at C-SPAN 3, and the clip and future updates will also be archived at C-SPAN.org.

"Congress is aware of and tracking all expenditures. The National

Guard, along with all branches of the military, is collecting victims and getting them off the streets and under cover. Emergency medical services are still available in case of serious illness or injury. A 900 number, strictly for victims of the occurrence, will be available on C-SPAN 3 by this evening so families can arrange to have victims relocated to a hospital or emergency medical facility. Again, we expect a high call volume so you can also go online and fill out a transportation request at http://www.patientpickup.gov. We are working to create a system for locating missing persons, but our first priority is for all victims to receive medical attention. In the meantime, we will collect identification and take photos of every patient to create a searchable database. Press Secretary Kenneth Mathews will keep you updated on all new developments.

"I am asking that all able-bodied medical personnel report to their local hospitals to volunteer their services. Once an infrastructure is in place, everyone will receive compensation for their time.

"Because we have no clue as to what caused the occurrence, Lilian Daniels, Director of NASA, will work with her scientists to rule out any space or atmospheric anomalies. One of their astronauts collapsed on the space station yesterday as well and NASA is arranging an emergency launch to retrieve him and bring him home.

"I have assigned Attorney General Allison Simmons as Legal Liaison for patient's rights and she will release footage of their care and accommodation. She will schedule press conferences as necessary to keep us updated on any issues or concerns.

"Dr. Anthony Lancaster, originally the director of Boston Mass, is now in charge of appointing a director for each tent city. He is working with FEMA to locate facilities for those victims in a coma as well as locating the medical equipment they need to take care of victims. The directors will report to Dr. Lancaster directly. I believe that he has already assigned Janeen Corbett to Boston and the surrounding hospitals and they are up and functioning.

"Last, I would like to introduce Walter Hickman, MD, Director of the Centers for Disease Control and Prevention (CDC). He will give you a current status report."

Walter Hickman walked to the podium and shook the President's hand. Short at just 5'8" tall, his suit looked too large for his small frame. His round metal-framed owl glasses made his dark brown eyes appear larger. His narrow mustache and thinning brown hair gave him a mousy appearance until he opened his mouth to speak. A small chuckle went through the room at the deep, confident voice that resonated throughout the room as he spoke.

"We are only in our initial testing phase. We can however rule out a bioterrorist attack. I have labeled this a pandemic because of the widespread epidemic that has affected so many people in so many countries. We are still not ruling out an airborne pathogen, although we do not believe that is the case, especially because one of our astronauts took ill. Also, an airborne pathogen would typically have affected many more people. We have a group of scientists from a variety of specialties who are collecting blood samples from a cross section of subjects. We are working backwards, so to speak, because we need to know what this occurrence *isn't* before we can ascertain what it *is*. I do want to assure you that no one is suffering any pain or discomfort. Every patient we have examined thus far has normal vital signs and other than their unconscious state, they are perfectly healthy. We will transport all pregnant women who are victims to their nearest maternity wards for special care. Additional care units for any special-needs pregnancies will be located in New York City, Boston, Maryland, Florida, Missouri,

Oklahoma, Texas, California, and Washington State."

Dr. Hickman rearranged his notes before continuing. "At this stage, we are doing everything possible to make sure victims are comfortable. We monitor their vital signs, and heart and brain activity; catheters are handling their waste, feeding tubes and IVs are inserted for nutrients. Nursing staff are repositioning patients at regular intervals to avoid complications such as decubitus ulcers—bedsores—and performing passive exercises to avoid muscle contractures and blood clots. Because of the vast numbers of victims, we will need extra personnel as well as volunteers to help care for them. The 900 number at the bottom of your screen is for those with any patient care experience willing to work with victims. When all phone lines are busy, you can apply online at our website: http://www.occurencepersonel.gov. We are implementing a thirty-two hour course for certification as a patient care assistant. Responsibilities include feeding, changing of catheter bags, IV bags, bedding, taking vital signs, repositioning, and passive exercise. For victims who have pre-existing conditions, there may be other medical care responsibilities. We estimate that at first, each caretaker may be responsible for the care of up to fifty victims and work three twelve hour shifts per week. These figures may change as more caretakers volunteer. We also need employees and volunteers for a variety of hospital and research duties and you will find a form on the website for that as well. Salaries are commensurate based on your location and the demand for personnel. Doctors will always be on staff for any other medical emergencies. We ask that any able-bodied retired physicians or physician's assistants, and medical students who are not already assigned residencies to please report to your nearest hospitals and emergency medical facilities.

"On another note, everyone will receive medical care regardless of their insurance carrier or medical plan. What personal insurance does not cover, the government will. We are forming a committee to work with insurance companies and state medical assistance programs.

"I want to assure you the minute we discover what has occurred and how to resolve this problem, we will inform the public as quickly as possible. Thank you."

Dr. Hickman stepped away from the podium and a tired-looking President once again shook his hand.

President Mitchell wiped his eyes wearily with a handkerchief, something he had never done in public before. The weight of the world was on his shoulders and you could see it in his face.

"That is all the information that I have for you right now. I know the public is anxious for information and we will notify you of further press briefings and introduce you to other government personnel who are hard at work as we speak. On a personal note, I want you to know that I am praying for each and every one of you. God Bless America."

Chapter 3

CDC Building, Washington, D.C., Friday, April 14, 2017, 7:00 p.m.

AS much as Janeen Corbett hated to fly, driving to Washington would take her seven hours, hours she couldn't afford to take away from the hospital. The past thirty-six hours had flown by and as she listened to the constant thump of the helicopter's blades, she found the sound soothing and she took the opportunity to close her eyes for a moment.

She was flying to Washington D.C. to meet with Dr. Anthony Lancaster, the director of Boston Mass, her boss for less than a week. She had finished her fellowship and Boston Mass snatched her up on her first interview. They wasted no time completing the paperwork and before she knew it, she had begun working less than two weeks after the interview. She was unsure as to why Dr. Lancaster would have chosen to make her the director of Boston Mass' eight tent cities, especially since she had never directed anything, not even a small medical practice, and was simply the newest doctor on staff at Boston Mass. She hadn't even had time to unpack her boxes in the house her parents had bought her as a graduation gift. But she felt it would be inappropriate to question Lancaster's authority. She knew that her father, Dr. Cole Corbett, a renowned plastic surgeon, had worked with Lancaster some years before in Doctors without Borders, but she doubted seriously that had anything to do with his decision. She had been unable to reach her parents since the occurrence because all cell towers were overwhelmed and her calls ended with a busy signal. Even using a landline was nearly impossible. She had finally sent a text message and then an e-mail to her parents, but she was unsure if either went through.

Janeen hoped the meeting would not be overly time consuming because she wanted to get back to the tent cities. When the helicopter took off, she looked down and saw military personnel constructing a barbed wire fence around the hospital and the tents. This concerned her, but apparently, tonight she would also meet her military liaison and find out exactly what the plans were for the hospital.

When the helicopter landed, she opened the door, ducked her head, and hurried over to shake Doctor Lancaster's hand.

African American, Lancaster had a youthful appearance, but she knew he had to be in his early sixties. Even so, he moved toward her with a runner's stride and stood ramrod straight, She had never seen him wear anything but scrubs and that is one of the reasons she accepted the position in the ER at Boston Mass. He was a director, but he was first and foremost a doctor and not afraid to get his hands dirty. She respected that.

He motioned for her to follow him away from the deafening noise and once inside the building, they could finally hear each other speak.

Dr. Lancaster placed his hand on her arm and indicated they should stay on the stairwell. "I know that you must be under a great deal of stress, which is why I selected you for this position. You trained in emergency medicine, the most stressful job in the hospital. I do have to warn you to expect some backlash from some staff who believe this assignment should be theirs."

"Yes, I've already run into a few of them today. I just kept it professional."

Dr. Lancaster smiled and for just a moment, she thought she caught a twinkle in his tired eyes.

"We are meeting with a group tonight. Normally it would be just us and our military liaison, but since I appointed you first and you have the B Mass facility nearly up and running, I thought this meeting could be informative. My job is to make sure all emergency facility and hospital directors have what they need and to keep them up-to-date on any progress we make regarding the occurrence. Also, Boston Mass will have test subjects and you may be working with the CDC/W directly. Let's head down and get you a cup of coffee before the meeting starts— you look like you need a pick-me-up."

* * *

After ordering them both a cup of strong, dark, bitter coffee, Dr. Lancaster gave her a brief tour of the facility. At the end of his tour, they arrived at a conference room and he walked in with confidence. Already seated around the table were six other people.

The most decorated officer in the room stood up. "Dr. Corbett, it is a pleasure to meet you despite these horrible circumstances. I'm General Harrison. Please allow me to introduce some of the people you will be working with."

A broad-shouldered man in his mid-thirties with clipped dark blond hair stood up. Tall, with broad shoulders, his piercing blue eyes seemed to look through her rather than at her.

"This is Colonel Martin Forester. He's in charge of the military and the emergency facilities for Massachusetts. He reports directly to me and I report to our President. Each state will have their own liaison and we will conference as needed when issues arise. Right now our biggest battle is enforcing martial law."

Colonel Forester shook Janeen's hand. "I'm sure that many of your questions will come up in the course of evening. If not, you can always ask. I have an open-door policy and if you need anything for the hospital or tents, please let me know," he said with a soft smile that revealed perfectly straight teeth. His face was a bit weatherbeaten, but it gave him an air of distinction.

"Your boss, Dr. Lancaster also reports directly to the president. The people in this room will work closely together to help solve the current situation. We not only need to determine the cause, but how to treat it," General Harrison said as he pulled out a chair for Janeen.

The general placed his hand on the shoulder of the man sitting on her right. "Walter Hickman is the director of the CDC as well as a renowned scientist in his field."

"How do you do?" Hickman said as he shook her hand.

Janeen found herself surprised at the baritone voice that came from this diminutive man.

The General walked around the table and stood beside a woman's chair. "The lovely lady with him is a genius and I am not engaging in flattery. Colleen Giles supervises all research that the CDC is doing at any given time. She is the director of research and development."

Janeen found the woman stunning. When Colleen stood to lean over and shake her hand, she had been surprised at the strength of her grip. The woman must be at least six feet tall and her flawless skin reminded Janeen of the porcelain dolls she had collected as a child—still did if she were honest with herself. A small indulgence she made once a year and they had to be antique porcelain.

The General went to stand next to a middle-aged woman who appeared nervous and out of place. This is Grace Langford; she represents

FEMA and is working with Dr. Lancaster as well as Dr. Hickman on emergency protocols.

"Lillian Daniels could not join us this evening as she is preparing the emergency launch to retrieve the astronaut who is in a coma. Now if we could get started, I know most of us are anxious to get down to work. I felt this meeting was necessary to familiarize ourselves with the hierarchy we'll establish and to go over all the information we do have and to discuss where some of our research is heading," General Harrison said as he took his own seat. "Lancaster, why don't you start?"

Dr. Lancaster opened his brief case and pulled out a handful of dossiers. "I will briefly summarize the information that I have just given you. Janeen is director of Boston Mass tent city. The hospital itself has 999 beds. We are going to make the rooms a bit more crowded and add another three hundred beds. We have a hundred private rooms and we are going to utilize that space. Our campus is large and Colonel Forester availed himself of every square inch—he placed eight tents connected together in a rather odd but satisfactory configuration. Total housing capability is five thousand two hundred and ninety-nine beds.

"If you turn to the next page there is a list of an additional twenty-five hospitals in Boston alone. Janeen has agreed to coordinate the information she receives between us and the directors of these tent cities as well. The following pages list the major hospitals in larger population areas and the directors of each facility. I am still in the process of working on the Midwest and West coast. This evening and tomorrow, I will be teleconferencing with the north portion of the state and then the southern assigned liaisons in California. I believe we are going to need to move thousands of victims to less crowded areas. Another thought is to use the enclosed Staple's Center, the Laker's stadium in Los Angeles. We could easily fit thirty to forty thousand bunk beds there, the problem would be personnel, but I am working on that as well," Lancaster smiled, but it didn't quite reach his eyes.

"Janeen, do you have anything in addition to add or have questions?" Lancaster asked.

"Why are they surrounding the hospital with barbed wire? It looks like an internment camp?"

"I can answer that, Janeen," Colonel Forester said turning to speak to her directly. "It is for the patient's security. As you know, we have had to declare martial law and even with calling home half our military forces and recalling all Guardsmen for duty it is a precarious situation. Hospitals have drugs and we need to make sure they stay there. I believe once we have again restored order the barbed wire fences will not be necessary, but at this point, we are not taking any chances."

Janeen nodded her head in understanding. "Another issue is EKG Machines. We called every clinic in Boston and could only collect three-hundred and fifty of them. Between storage and what we had in the building that adds an additional fourteen hundred."

"The President is encouraging medical equipment companies to produce them as quickly as possible, but until they arrive you'll need to dedicate nurses or nursing assistants to do nothing but take vitals," Lancaster explained. "The other medical supplies you'll need will arrive tomorrow at 0600. Colonel Forester has the manifest and if you need additional supplies you can compile a list and give it to him."

"Another thing that needs to be addressed is physical therapy for the sleepers. We have a shortage of physical therapists in the Boston area for our purposes, but many nurses have training in passive exercise for neuropatients. I think we need some dialogue between the two as we organize volunteers for all duties.

"I think I'll leave my part on a positive note," Janeen said with a bright smile. "Two hundred doctors have reported to Boston Mass and three hundred nurses. There are also over a hundred military medics who have reported, as well. Once new employees are onboard and we've trained the new patient care assistants and volunteers, I think all of the victims' immediate needs will be covered. I believe we could reasonably send a hundred nurses to another facility if they are in need."

"Excellent," the General said gruffly. "We have already received over twenty-five thousand applications for patient care assistants and technicians of varying specialties and over fifty thousand volunteer applications. We have our data people dividing them up into areas and you should have a list by morning.

"Dr. Hickman, can you give us any news or insight about what direction the CDC is taking?"

"We can say with a hundred percent certainty that this is not a bioterrorism attack, at least not one we are familiar with. If—and I spell that with a capital I—this is bioterrorism, it is something beyond our current understanding and we have some of the greatest scientists in the world working at the CDC. We are slowly ruling causes out and will try to replicate the occurrence by using blood from a cross section of victims. Our dilemma is that this may have nothing to do with blood or a viral disease. Janeen, we are sending scientists to Boston Mass first to perform a variety of tests because Boston is ground zero, so to speak."

"Excuse me Dr. Hickman; I think we should also discuss the coma theory. There's a vast difference of opinion as to the validity of this approach, but we must pursue every possible model," Colleen said with enthusiasm.

"That is just a theory at this point and until we have something viable to put on the table, we are going to bypass this discussion. General, our teams are working on a large variety of experiments and research and we have nothing positive to report at this time. I will keep you and Dr. Lancaster updated on any new verified information," Dr. Hickman said.

Dr. Giles frowned at Dr. Hickman, but remained silent.

"You should be aware that we are working with other scientists across the world on a solution or an explanation for the occurrence. These scientists are from the European Union, Germany, France, and Switzerland, and Holland to name a few. The solution lies in science and we are going to find it."

"I hope the answers come soon, Dr. Lancaster, because I'm not sure how long we can treat people in these vegetative states without more sophisticated health care." the General stated.

Chapter 4

JANEEN woke up with crick in her neck and cursed the cots the hospital had placed in the staff lounge. After tossing and turning, she had finally fallen asleep and gotten a whole five hours of sleep. She decided that if she took a twenty-minute power nap from time to time, she could manage. That's what sustained her through her residency.

As Janeen removed the towel to step into a hot shower, she glanced down at her body and smiled in satisfaction. Her years of running college track had kept her tone and fit and she had runner's legs, lean but powerful. Her straight black hair brushed her shoulders and she pulled it back into a ponytail as she always did when she worked in the hospital.

She stepped into the hot water and let it ease her too tight muscles. As she lathered soap on her honey brown skin, a mixture of her mother's black skin and her father's Irish background, she let the water sooth her tense muscles. Janeen had never had the insecurities that most adolescents go through. She had never had acne and her vibrant green eyes always sparkled with enthusiasm, humor, and intelligence. As she washed her face, she smiled remembering how her father had always told her that her high cheekbones spoke of nobility.

Her concern about her parents was growing and she felt guilty for not calling them when she arrived to her new home, but Colonel Forester said that she could use his satellite phone to try to reach them today.

Her mother taught economics at Dartmouth and her father was a well-known cosmetic surgeon for the rich and vain. That seemed like a cruel analysis because he did enjoy his work and it gave him the time and funds to donate to Doctors Without Borders. He favored helping children born with cleft palates and other deformities. She found herself grateful that he hadn't been traveling this week.

Janeen was extremely close to both her vivacious mother and her more introverted father. A smile crossed her face as she thought of him. Supposedly he'd given up smoking his pipe the day she came into the world, but he still carried it around with him wherever he went and on occasion when he held her she could smell the cherry tobacco and it made her feel safe and loved. She remembered as a child crawling up into his lap for her goodnight story and his vest smelled so good, the sweet smoke clinging to him. He still wore those vests, along with the bowtie. He was a quaint man and whenever she looked at him, she could read the love in his eyes for both her and her mother.

Louise, her mother, was a powerhouse. She not only taught economics, but also organized volunteers to transform a vacant field in their neighborhood into a community garden that supplied produce to the local farmers market. She was forever rallying for one cause or another and stayed busy during campaigns, attending meetings, and handing out flyers.

Though Janeen's parents were opposites personality-wise, the love they shared was an unbreakable bond, a friendship with just the right amount of passion mixed in. They were an abnormally close family and often took their vacations together, although Louise was always trying to fix Janeen up with one of her students. But she rarely dated because her work dominated her life. She had hoped when she took the position at Boston Mass after the hectic months of her residency that her work schedule would slow down a bit.

"Yeah, right," she whispered as she tied her tennis shoes. Who would have known that a pandemic was coming and would consume her world?

Janeen had called an early morning staff meeting, first with the nurses, then the doctors, which Colonel Forester would attend. If possible, she wanted to start interviews with potential patient care assistants and health care workers from a variety of fields. There was a 2:00 p.m. conference call with all the local Boston hospitals and she didn't expect that would go over smoothly either. Some senior physicians here at Boston Mass made it very clear they resented her position and her inexperience and she expected the same reception of the other tent city directors.

There was a knock on the doctor's lounge door and Janeen called out that they should come in. The moment the door opened, the most wonderful scent entered. Rosemary Stiles, the nursing director, entered wearing a smile and carrying a plate of homemade blueberry muffins.

From the first day she had worked here, Rosemary had instantly become her friend and Janeen found her vocabulary delightful. She shot from the hip and swore like a sailor. She had an opinion about everything and could convince you that she was correct in her assumptions even when they were preposterous. She was a jovial woman in her early fifties. Her body reflected her spirit, short, round, and a cuddly shape. She obviously liked eating her cooking as much as she liked making them.

"I know you're not eating the way you are supposed to so I've appointed myself your personal nutritionist."

Rosemary's husband had fallen victim during the occurrence and she had put him in a bed closest to the nursing station. Despite her concern over his welfare, Rosemary had maintained her sense of humor, and when Janeen walked by his room she could often hear Rosemary carrying on a one-sided conversation with him.

"I set one next to Jack's bed. If my cooking doesn't wake him up, nothing will. That's the reason he married me. He fell in love with my cooking first and me second."

Janeen laughed as she reached over and took a muffin. "They're still warm."

"I'm using the cafeteria ovens—just wait till you see what I'm making for lunch," she teased.

"I'm glad you're here. I wanted to talk to you before our meeting. I've done a lot of thinking about this . . . I think it would be best if you formed a committee of ten or fifteen nurses and interviewed the potential candidates for the patient care assistant positions. They will be working under your supervision and I trust your judgment."

"A soldier dropped off a package for you this morning, probably the applications."

"I'm just wondering how we are going to do background checks— we don't have access to the Internet anymore. I'm telling you, it's the goddamn government who shut it off. They're taking over everything and I don't trust them. Course that Colonel Forester could warm my bed any time he wanted," Rosemary said with an exaggerated wink.

Janeen began to laugh and Rosemary joined in, her laughter loud and boisterous.

"I don't think the government had anything to do with the Internet. I think every single person with a computer is trying to figure out what happened and that's bogging down the Internet. Theories are flying around and some of them are ludicrous, but people have to find something to hold on to and I think the unknown is worse.

"Back to the interviews. According to the General, they pre-screened all applicants before they sent them to us. We need to hire two hundred and fifteen of them. Many of the applicants may choose to volunteer rather going through the training program. We will divide them up so they each care for fifty victims during two shifts. That should free up the nurses to change catheters, give feedings, and take care of anyone who is sick while the assistants monitor the vitals and reposition the patients. We will also train them on passive physical therapy."

"Talking about sick, we have thirty-nine women in the maternity ward. One of them is due any day. We have five obstetricians and three pediatricians who showed up.

"I'm not trying to be negative, but what are we going to do if they don't wake up?"

"I honestly don't know; I'm trying not to think about it yet. I just want to make sure we can take care of them now. We'll worry what to do when all our bases are covered."

Janeen stood up and stretched her limbs. "I forgot to tell you—the CDC is sending some scientists here to do random testing on the victims. A doctor will accompany each one to offer any assistance they might need."

"Everyone is waiting for us in the cafeteria and I'm not trying to hurt your feelings, but you look like shit. You can't take care of anyone if you fall ill yourself," Rosemary chastised.

Janeen blinked at Rosemary's concern. "I'll be fine. Your delicious food along with more power naps will get me back on my feet. Let's not keep them waiting."

Chapter 5

Boston Mass, Saturday, April 15, 2017, 7:00 a.m.

BEFORE reaching the cafeteria, Janeen could hear raised voices and knew this meeting wasn't going to go as smoothly as she had hoped.

Rosemary entered the cafeteria first and the room became dead silent. When Janeen walked to the front of the room, she could hear the whispering behind her. The nurses would want answers and she had few to give them.

Janeen turned around, took a deep breath, and began to speak. "Thank you all for coming in so early. I know that everyone is in shock after Thursday's occurrence and I am afraid I don't have the answers you are looking for. As of now, we don't know what caused people to collapse and there is no known medical reason why they haven't awakened. The CDC is working around the clock with scientists all over the world to find the answers."

"How many victims are there," someone shouted out.

"In the US, thirty-five million. Worldwide, approximately eleven percent of the population. The occurrence affected the entire world and that's one of the reasons they don't believe it was a bioterrorist attack. They have eliminated the possibility of an airborne pathogen due to the selective nature of those infected. Our priority as health professionals is to take care of the victims until we can find out some answers. The world is in shock, but we don't have the luxury of grieving right now."

A woman wearing a nurse's smock stood up and tears flowed down her face. "I shouldn't even be here. Both my children and my husband . . ." She broke down and began to sob as she took her seat.

"I know that each and every one of you have suffered a personal tragedy and being here is voluntary . . ."

"What about our families? We've filled out the form for them to be picked up and we haven't had any response. My neighbor is watching over my father and mother so I could be here."

"If you feel more comfortable staying home with your loved ones, it's perfectly understandable and no one would blame you for that decision. If you would prefer to have your affected family members here, Rosemary will hand you a form and the Colonel will make arrangements so we can begin picking them up this afternoon. I'd like to tell you that this situation is temporary, but I don't have the answer as to how long this will last or even what it is.

"If you choose to continue working, give your name to Rosemary and we'll develop a schedule. Those with family members in the hospital will have priority to choose their shift. Right now, the hospital is in lockdown except for the movement of necessary personnel. That is going to change however, once we've set up and people can search the database of sleepers. At that point, we'll have to develop visitation schedule for families to visit their loved ones."

A man stood up and placed his hands on his hips. "This is all just fine and dandy, but I don't even know where the hell my husband and two children are at."

"A database is in progress so that you can check online to locate them. It will be another three to four days before it is operational. I know that isn't the answer you were looking for, but we have to be patient until the government can get organized.

"Because we are under martial law, until the streets are clear of looters, an Army bus will pick you up, deliver you to the hospital, and take you home once your shift is over.

"We are attempting to contact cafeteria workers to see if they will come back to work. We will provide all meals free of charge . . ."

Rosemary's loud voice drowned out the talking in the room. "If they don't come in, I'll do the cooking myself."

Applause and laughter filled the room and the mood in the room lightened. Rosemary stood up and took a bow.

"I've asked Rosemary to form a committee to interview potential health care personnel to help with the victims. Since they'll be working under your supervision, I felt it best that you be the ones who hire them. I know that you are running around trying to do everything you can, but the job is impossible without some help. We are going to hire two hundred and fifteen, which we will divide between two shifts. I know we are short EKG machines and the government is doing all they can to get more, but until then, we are going to have to do this the old-fashioned way."

"How do we determine who gets the machines?" a voice shouted out.

"Excellent point, I would say the elderly and the youngest. We will take everyone else's vitals every two to three hours."

The room groaned and Janeen didn't blame them for their frustrations.

"Now, I'm going to share even worse news, depending on your point of view. Our emergency room has fifty beds—we are going to add another fifty and start taking emergency cases beginning at 2:00 p.m. today. You are going to see military personnel at every entrance of the hospital and on every floor of the hospital. They are here for our protection, even though I admit it is an uncomfortable situation. Medical supplies will arrive today and Rosemary will assign a group to keep track of what we need so she can reorder them."

"What about the barbed wire around the hospital? It's intimidating to say the lease," a young woman near the back of the room waved her hands to get Janeen's attention.

"That is there for your protection as well. Hospitals carry drugs and with all the civil unrest they want to make sure we have a safe work environment. I'll admit it freaked me out when I saw it as well, but now that I understand the rationale, it gives me a sense of security."

Janeen searched the room trying to make eye contact with as many as she could when she noticed Colonel Forester standing in the back of the room. She motioned him to come to the front and he made his way through the crowd to join her.

"I would like to introduce you to Colonel Forester. He is in charge of all military personnel in Massachusetts as well as the tent cities."

"Good morning," he said, his deep voice resonating through the room. "I've been listening to your concerns and want you to know we will address them as quickly as possible. For those of you with families at home, we will begin to pick them up immediately. We have received bunk bed shipments all night long and have enough for the tents. We were also able to confiscate another five hundred EKG machines, which should make your job easier.

"Until your kitchen is up and running again, you're welcome to eat in our mess tent, although I have to be honest, nothing is going to compare to Rosemary's blueberry muffins. Please address all your concerns in writing to Dr. Corbett and she will pass them on to me.

"I just want to assure you that we are doing everything possible to find out what happened and to reverse it. The positive news is the victims are healthy and don't appear to be in any immediate danger. Of course, there were victims with prior medical conditions and we are doing our best to discover and treat those. You will have heard the term sleepers used to refer to them and it's as good a moniker as anything else. Let's just work together to find out a way to wake them up."

"Excuse me, Colonel," Rosemary said. "We'll have a list of people for the interviews within the hour."

"I'll send over my communications specialist and we will contact them and start picking them up at 2:00 p.m. How many do you think you can interview today?"

"We will have fifteen nurses interviewing them so I would say a hundred today and the rest tomorrow."

"Excellent, I know how much you need the help. Now, if you have no further questions, I need to borrow Dr. Corbett for a bit."

"I'm going to leave you in Rosemary's capable hands. She has the pickup forms and will work with you on an interview committee and to schedule shifts."

As Janeen and Colonel Forester left the cafeteria, they could hear nurses calling out questions to Rosemary.

* * *

"I think you handled the nurse's meeting quite well," Colonel Forester said as they left the cafeteria.

"They're scared and confused and they have good reason to be. The best thing for everyone is to keep busy doing something productive. I'm thinking of the millions of people sitting in their homes listening to news reports and trying to surf the Internet and contact loved ones. They are driving themselves crazy with frustration by this point."

"That's why our first priority is to restore order and collect the bodies in the streets. The sooner people get back to a semi-normal schedule the better off they will be. We have no idea if the sleepers will wake up and we need to take people's minds off it at this point."

"Colonel, I told the nurses we could relocate their family members today."

"I will ask my communications officer to make the arrangements and since we are working together. Why don't you call me Forester?"

"You can call me Janeen. Thank you with you help in there, I think you gave them a sense of reassurance."

"Janeen, I stopped by this morning to give you a satellite phone. I know you need to contact the other hospitals as well as Dr. Lancaster and the phone lines are overloaded.

"Also, I'm holding a Skype conference call with all area hospitals at 2:00 p.m. Do you want to participate? Visiting each hospital at this point would be difficult because of all the checkpoints."

"That's an excellent idea, I'd planned to contact them at 2:00 p.m. myself. Thank you so much for the phone."

"When you're ready, just tell the soldier on duty outside the main entrance and he will bring you to the communications tent."

* * *

Janeen took the phone and went to her office for privacy. Stacks of boxes stood like pillars and she had to weave her way around them until she reached her desk chair. She moved the box of porcelain dolls off the desk and powered up her computer. She checked her e-mail, but couldn't get an Internet connection. With trembling fingers, she dialed her parent's home number.

It picked up on the second ring.

"Janeen, is that you?" Her father asked in a horse whisper.

"Oh Dad, I'm glad I finally got you, I've been worried sick. Are you okay?" Janeen said in a rush.

"As well as can be expected under the current circumstances. Your mother and I were having breakfast on Thursday morning; we were watching the news and saw the first people collapse. I turned to look at your mother and her eyes grew wide just before she collapsed. Janeen, I saw the fear on her face—she knew what was happening to her."

Janeen felt tears running down her cheeks and it took her a moment before she could speak. "I was so worried about both of you. Mom is such a strong woman and I know she is going to pull through this.

"Dad, are you sure she was aware of what was going on?"

"I've been married to your mother for thirty-five years and whatever happened scared her. I could read it on her face. Anyway, I went to the surgical center, borrowed an EKG machine, and brought it home. She hasn't responded, but her vital signs are strong. No one had shown up for work and I haven't been able to contact anyone else from the center.

"A few of the neighbors have shown up and asked me to look at their loved ones and I did examine them, but there's nothing I can do to help at this point."

"Dad, why don't you bring Mom here to the hospital in case of any complications? Also, the CDC is going to be testing patients here so she'd be closer to a cure and possibly she could be in the first test group."

"No, I want to take care of her myself. I wouldn't be good for anyone else at this point—this is where I belong. I intubated her, but my supplies won't last long.

"Janeen as a physician, I'm not going to have them experimenting on your mother, we will wait until the cure is perfected."

"I understand dad, but promise me you will reconsider. I can't stand knowing my mother is in a coma. As far as the supplies, I'll have them delivered to you today. What about you? How are you doing?"

"I'm in shock like the rest of the world. Your mother is my primary concern. I sat glued to the television for hours to listen for information and finally had to turn it off because all it was doing was making me worry more." He stopped speaking for a moment and Janeen knew he was trying not to cry. When he pulled himself together, he changed the topic.

"This pandemic, according to the news, is still a mystery."

"Yes, we haven't discovered anything except it is not an airborne virus. I'm working with the CDC and they're stumped at this point."

Janeen explained her new position and told him everything she'd learned so far.

"Dr. Lancaster is correct, you are the perfect person for this job, but I know you, Janeen; you'll work yourself sick. Promise me you'll take care of yourself and get enough rest and nutrition."

"I promise, Dad!" Janeen grinned at his admonishment. He had said the same thing when she was an intern. "I have a meeting with the hospital doctors, but I'll have the food you need delivered today and I will give you a call this evening. I love you and kiss mom for me."

"I love you too, sweetie. Don't worry about your mom; I'm taking good care of her."

"Dad, how many EKG machines are still at the surgical center? We desperately need them."

"There are still seven of them there. The hospital is welcome to them."

"We could use every one we can get our hands on. I'll let you know when we're ready to pick them up."

"When they deliver the food I will give them the keys. I don't want to leave your mother alone. Also, I removed all the narcotics from the center in case of a break in, if the hospital needs them I have them all packed up."

"I think we're alright on drugs so you can hold on to them. Dad, I have to run. I love you and I know mom is going to pull out of this."

Chapter 6

Burbank, California, Saturday, April 15, 2017, 8:00 a.m.

NATHANIEL Long stood at the end of the long conference table with fists clenched in frustration. His thick, dyed black hair, which under normal circumstances appeared perfectly coiffed, stood out in all directions from him running his hands through it in frustration. He had begun his mission as the evangelist at Los Angeles Outreach and Gospel church twenty years ago. The Lord had been preparing him his entire life for the end times and Satan was putting roadblocks in his way.

Bob Jacobs, the head deacon, tried to diffuse the situation with reason. "Nathaniel, by executive order, the government confiscated the Staples Center and the Orange Bowl as well as all the other large venues to house the victims of the occurrence. We are under martial law, there's a six o'clock curfew and no way will they make an exception for a revival meeting."

"The Lord spoke to me and gave me a message for the world and I will not fail Him. By the blood of His son's hands and feet as he hung on the cross is the only way the world will find redemption. There are so many souls that need saving, even those that believe their redeemed need to hear this message. People say they believe, but they don't really understand what real faith is about. It's easy to praise God when your life is going well, but this is going to be a time when their faith has to sustain them through the darkest of hours."

"We can contact all the local television stations and radio stations. We will use what is in the building fund to pay for ads if we have to," Bob said with conviction.

"Fine, we will hold a 10:00 a.m. service and put speakers in the parking lot for those we don't have room for. How many does the church hold?"

"With the recent addition of the balcony, thirty-five hundred. Our membership stands at close to seven thousand.

"What do you want me to do with Sister Ellen's body? Should we call and have her body picked up? It's hard to believe she is in a coma."

"She is no longer Sister Ellen Bob. Put her in a chair beside the pulpit and tie her up so she stays in place."

Nathaniel took a moment to smooth back his hair and straighten his tie. "We have to reach the world, Bob. Their time is almost up and they must be saved by the blood of the lamb before it's too late."

"Can you share the message?"

"I can't, Bob. It would put you in mortal danger, and I won't take that chance. But what I do want is to get the flock to make as many signs as possible. The time is almost nigh, it is time for us to fall on our knees and ask for God's redemption."

"So I am the shepherd?"

"Yes. Amanda Franklin is in charge of the ladies' Bible study and I'm sure that this is the perfect job for her. Frank Jenkins may begin the prayer chain so every member will understand the importance of coming to tomorrow's service. I want all the deacons and faithful followers to be on the phones sharing the good news."

"Is there anyone else to contact?"

Nathaniel raised his eyes as though conferring with heaven. "Yes. Speak with Judith Baxter, the director of the church choir; I want to raise the roof off this building tomorrow with songs of praise and glory. Lastly, I want as many television and radio interviews I can get before tomorrow morning. Pay to have our Sunday ad bombard the airwaves and to have our service broadcast to those unable to attend."

"I'll get right on it, Brother Nathaniel. Is there anything else I can do to help you?"

"Thank you Bob, but I must bear this weight alone, just as Jesus carried the cross. Are the other preparations ready for tomorrow's service?"

"I followed your instructions to the letter. I know you've explained it to me, but I am weak in the flesh."

Nathaniel tried not to look at Bob in disgust. His sin was gluttony and the buttons on his shirt strained as if they might pop off at any minute. Chastising himself for not loving Bob despite his flaws, he took Bob's hands in his own. "The Lord knows that, Bob. But in the last hours, your faith will rise up and God's strength will help you to complete your tasks. Now if you will leave me, I need to pray."

As soon as Bob left the room, Nathaniel put aside his crutches and lay prostrate before the cross holding up the Son of God. His mother raised him from the time he was a child to study God's word and explained he was different because the Lord had special plans for him. Jesus had called her home last year and his only regret is that she wouldn't be here to share in this glorious moment with him and his followers.

Nathaniel knew he was different from other children growing up and that is why his mother had homeschooled him. When he asked her why God would not heal him, she explained that it was God's will and he had a greater purpose. Suffering from muscular dystrophy, he had worn leg braces from an early age and often found himself in a wheelchair. He always stood behind a specially designed pulpit that would hide his braces. His mother had claimed he was a special child and since a young age he wore black tailored suits and growing up, children had called him an undertaker. Instead of hurting his feelings, it made him feel empowered because it was God's will. Nathaniel had followed God's word to the letter. He had brought not even a sip of alcohol to his lips and he had remained a virgin, pure in the eyes of the Lord. Women had tried to tempt him, but with God's strength, he resisted them. The men were no better, whores in the sight of the Lord, they had wanted to fornicate with him too, but God had his own special punishment for their sins. For many it was too late, but when they heard God's words tomorrow, they would lie before the Lord and repent of their sins. God understood the weakness of the flesh and they would have one last chance to repent before he came to take them home. The apocalypse was mere days away and as their pastor, he must prepare them for the coming. People had been waiting for the end time for thousands of years and Nathaniel knew that God had waited for him to be ready to spread the good news.

He was a normal man and he felt the temptation of sin, but God had shown him how to slay those demons.

Nathaniel got up and locked all the church doors so he could be alone with his God. He removed his shirt and retrieved a small box behind the pulpit. He opened the box and lovingly took out the cat o' nine tails. He touched each knot on the strands of leather and felt God's love flowing through him. Satan's demons had no power over him and as he hit his back with the first lash, he cried out in satisfaction and pain.

Chapter 7

JANEEN heard her name called over the loudspeaker, requesting her to come to the hospital's main doors. When she arrived, there were two guards sandwiching a young girl wearing a long-sleeved shirt and a long skirt that looked as if she hadn't washed them in quite a while. Nor her hair, which hung in long, stringy clumps around her acne-covered her face. She held a white bible clasped firmly in both hands as if she expected someone to steal it from her.

"Dr. Corbett, this young woman said she is here to volunteer, but won't give us her home address or a phone number to call a guardian," the tallest guard said.

"It's alright; I'll take her with me," Janeen said softly and stepped back from the doors so the girl could enter.

"I'm Dr. Corbett, but you can call me Janeen. What's your name?"

"I'm Laureen Spellman and I came to pray for the sleepers. I could help in other ways too."

"How old are you, Laureen?"

"I'm a week away from my seventeenth birthday and I can tell by the way you're looking at me that you feel sorry for me. Well don't. I'm a foster kid for another week and then I'm on my own. I can take care of myself and God looks after me."

"Do your foster parents know you are here?"

"It's a group home and everyone pretty much comes and goes when they please. As long as we are there when the social worker visits we don't have to report to anyone."

"Well, we can use all the volunteers we can get. Why don't you come with me and let's get you fixed up."

Janeen walked beside Laureen, who watched the floor in front of her and refused to make eye contact. She took the girl to the doctors' lounge and spoke in a soft voice so as not to frighten the girl any more than she already was. Janeen went to the cupboard and pulled out a pair of green scrubs.

"These look like they might fit. Why don't you take a shower and change into these. All the technicians and patient care assistants we are hiring are going to wear them."

"Are you offering me a job?" Laureen stammered.

"Why yes, I am. It pays minimum wage, but you also receive room and board. Once you've changed, I will introduce you to Rosemary—she's the director of nursing here. I'm sure you'll get along fine with her. So what do you say?"

"I could really use the money, but I don't know how to take care of anyone."

Janeen smiled. "We have a training course starting tomorrow and until we get the bedding situation figured out, you can sleep in the nurse's lounge."

Laureen looked at Janeen distrustfully and held her Bible closer to her chest.

"Look, I'm sure you are as freaked out about what's happened as the rest of the world is. I'm offering you the chance to earn money and help people while you do it. What do you say?"

"I already have my GED," Laureen said defensively.

"All the better," Janeen said with a smile. "Is it a deal?"

"Yes, but I just want you to know I'm a hard worker and I don't take handouts."

"Believe me, you will earn your wage, and you might discover you enjoy the nursing field."

Laureen looked as if she wanted to smile but caught herself, but she relaxed and held the Bible at her side.

"Alright, I have a bit of paperwork to finish, so go ahead and get your shower and we'll go and try to find Rosemary. She's not difficult to find, she talks rather loudly."

Janeen pulled a travel kit from a cabinet and handed Laureen a toothbrush, comb, a towel, and a washcloth.

A half hour later when Laureen returned, her face was rosy from the hot shower and she looked like the young woman she was supposed to be. She couldn't believe that the state was going to emancipate this girl before she turned eighteen. She had other priorities to deal with right now, but she was going to find a way to help Laureen.

Janeen reached the cafeteria twenty minutes before her meeting with the doctors. The smell coming from the kitchen made her mouth water. When she entered the kitchen, she watched as Rosemary pulled out two cookie sheets of chocolate chip cookies.

"Rosemary, what in the world are you doing?" Janeen laughed.

"I know doctors and they can be arrogant assholes. They aren't going to be as nice as the nurses were and I know how to soften them up. My double chocolate chip cookies. It works every time. Here, you'd best eat one now, once the vultures descend it's every man for himself."

Rosemary gave Laureen a spatula and she shyly selected the smallest cookie on the baking sheet. When the teen returned the spatula, Rosemary swiftly moved the others to a plate on a countertop.

Janeen wrapped her arm around Laureen's shoulders and she immediately stiffened. "I'd like to introduce you to Laureen Spellman; she's our first official hired patient care assistant. We're going to provide her room and board as well."

Rosemary raised her eyebrows and took over. "Excellent. You can help me finish making the cookies and tomorrow we'll start your training. Today you can shadow me and get the lay of the land."

"Thank you," Laureen stammered. "I know how to cook and I'd be glad to help you finish baking."

"I would appreciate the help," Rosemary smiled brightly.

"Doc, the nurses are going through the applications for patient care assistants and should have them to the communications officer by noon. I've already sent over the list of people they need to pick up and we have a rotating schedule worked out for the next two weeks. You see, Doc, I delegate, stops me from going crazy. They are already on duty and half are changing feeding tubes and the other half are switching out IV bags and catheters. The rest of them are taking vitals. I hope you don't mind, but I scheduled the ER nurses on the same shift they were already on. I just added twenty of them and if that's not enough, I can always pull more nurses from the tent city. It's going to be a madhouse in there when people find out we're open. I called all the local ambulances and told them we'd be taking emergency patients. They told me the 911 numbers are going crazy."

"Rosemary, you are one amazing woman!"

"Nope, I've just been a nurse for the past twenty-five years and I've learned how to play the system. By the way, I reached the cafeteria manager and they'll be here at 11:00 a.m. to start cooking. The military guys are giving them their own private escort. Ethel, the head chef, seemed relieved to have something to do. She's a talker when she starts; I finally had to declare an emergency to get her off the phone."

Janeen began to laugh and Rosemary held out a plate of cookies.

When Janeen took a bite of her cookie, Laureen began to self-consciously nibble on hers.

Janeen smiled and wiped a crumb from the corner of her mouth, "These are delicious, what's your secret?"

"I use dark chocolate, it's better for you anyway, less fattening too . . . I should probably warn you about some of the docs you'll be talking with today."

"That's ok. Dr. Lancaster gave me a full report, and besides, half of them have found some reason or other to seek me out and check me out. They all have much to gossip about—I thought nurses were the ones who did that!"

"Oh we gossip alright, only difference is we tell the truth when we're doing it. So tell me Doc, what's really going on in the world? Rumors are flying and people are a lot more scared than they're letting on."

"Rosemary, as soon as we figure it out, I promise you'll be one of the first I talk to. The CDC will be showing up within the next few to do some testing. I think their biggest fear is that the occurrence will start again. The government doesn't like not having answers."

"My Henry, he's a tough old coot. I know he's going to pull out of this. I'm not sure what happened—hell, maybe it was the fuckin' aliens. They've been watching us this whole time anyway." Rosemary wiped her nose on a tissue and turned around so Janeen and Laureen couldn't see her face.

"You go on and take them plates of cookies out there. I already have pitchers of cold milk waiting."

Janeen reached out and patted Rosemary's shoulder. "You're one in a million and if I'm not careful you're going to make me fat."

Rosemary sniffled and managed a small smile. "You could use a few pounds on you; now get on out of here. Laureen and I need to get acquainted. She needs some fattening up as well."

When Janeen pushed open the door to the cafeteria, she could see that almost twenty doctors had arrived early. She held up the two plates of cookies and smiled. "Rosemary sends her best."

She recognized the Assistant Director, Dr. Hammons, and he wasn't smiling. He resented her for being in charge of the tent city since she had no experience. His meticulous dark grey suit stood out among a small group of doctors wearing casual clothes and lab coats. They quit talking when they saw her.

Janeen watched as one by one, they made their way towards the table. Those she didn't know introduced themselves and shook her hand. Before long, there was only standing room left and she went to the front of the room.

"Good morning. I can't tell you how much I appreciate all of you volunteering to help in this time of crisis. My name is Janeen Corbett and I am the tent city director while Dr. Lancaster works with the CDC and is a liasion to hospitals across the US as we deal with this situation. We have a lot to discuss this morning, but before we get started, I want to tell you what I do know about Thursday's occurrence.

"Honestly, the CDC doesn't know much. They will be here tomorrow to do a cross section of tests on sleepers. So far, the sleepers are healthy—if originally healthy—and their vital signs are strong. We can be grateful that this wasn't a bioterrorist attack. There are many other theories going around, but I won't speculate on those. As soon as I have more facts, you will know as quickly as possible."

"Why the military presence?" an older doctor asked.

"Boston is the ground zero of the occurrence, thus Boston Mass is a critical facility. Our state national guard as well as the national military is setting up headquarters in Massachusetts. Also, they are concerned about possible looting or gang interference because hospitals and pharmacies have supplies of narcotics and other drugs that could be sold on the street. They will escort any employee or volunteer here to their homes if you feel unsafe. I know some of you are staying at the hospital because you have family here and that is fine as well."

Janeen cleared her throat and reminded herself that these doctors didn't have to like her—they only needed to respect her and she would pull her friends close and her worst critic closer, as the old adage went.

"Dr. Hammonds, as Assistant Director of Boston Mass, you're familiar with how Dr. Lancaster runs the hospital and I'll depend on you to assist me as you have assisted him in running the tent city. I know the vast majority of the hospital is now filled with sleepers and this complicates your job even further. He speaks highly of you and I hope you'll become my right hand as well. Working together, I know we can through this cataclysmic event. The nurses are working on duty rosters, but if you could go over it and then arrange for all hospital personnel to get a copy and also work on the Doctors schedules it would be appreciated."

Dr. Hammonds unfolded is arms and puffed out his chest. "I am available for any help you need. I do have one suggestion . . ."

"Please go ahead," Janeen said with sincerity.

"I think we should keep the youngest and the oldest sleepers in the hospital and closest to the hospital in the first tent. They are the ones we should be most cautious with as they are the most vulnerable."

"I concur. If you will select twenty or so volunteers to help you to tag their beds, we can arrange for orderlies to move them before we admit more sleepers. The military is collecting those who have collapsed and those we've received pickup calls for and it would make it easier to move them before new sleepers arrive."

"I'll take care of it," he said with the slightest smile.

Janeen nodded her appreciation and continued. "We are reopening the emergency room at 2:00 p.m. today. The other hospitals will open theirs tomorrow. We've added another fifty beds and increased the nursing staff. I know everyone has had emergency room training, but do we have any specialists with us?" A dozen hands went up and Janeen sighed with relief. "That's a good start; we need another twenty doctors to volunteer. We'll work in twelve-hour shifts. It's going to get crowded in there, but we want to get patients in and out again as quickly as possible."

"Excuse me," a young woman said, holding up her hand. "I'm Dr. Fields. Dr. Andrews, who is in charge of the emergency room, is one of the sleepers. I've been training under him and I would be glad to get a roster prepared if those willing to volunteer would join me after the meeting."

"That would be helpful, Dr. Fields, I appreciate the effort. If you could just post the roster on the bulletin board once you compile a list."

"I know that not all of you are on staff here and I will need you to fill out the employment forms—it's just a formality for insurance. I can't tell you how much I appreciate all of you being here in this crisis."

"Dr. Corbett, my name is Dan Caddell and I'm an obstetrician. I have a few sleepers on the maternity ward, floor five, and one is due this week. We're going to need to perform a C-section. I see five other obstetricians here and we need to exam all pregnant women as soon as possible. We don't know what effect this could have on their un-born children and I believe we should perform an ultrasound on each mother as well as an amniocentesis."

"Dr. Caddell, if I could ask you to head the committee for that floor, I would appreciate it. If you need any additional medical equipment, please let me know. Also, if you coordinate with Rosemary you can select the nurses who are familiar with deliveries and the surgical teams.

"Do we have any anesthesiologists with us today?"

A dozen hands went up in the air.

"Excellent. Please work out your own schedules so the hospital has enough of you to go around on each shift.

"I need to ask the rest of you to examine all five thousand sleepers and take note of any anomalies you find. We've never had anything like this happen before and I know it's a long and tedious project. We'll start with the youngest and eldest sleepers first. Our greatest challenge is going to be those on medications with prior medical conditions. It is my hope they all have ID and have been seen here at the hospital at one time or another . . ."

"And what are you going to do while we're doing all this," Dr. Hammonds asked snidely.

"I'm responsible for organizing the operations of all twenty-five tent cities in the Boston area. I will work from here so I'm always avail-able."

"I know you have family members you are concerned about and Colonel Forester will relocate them here to the hospital today if you would like. Rosemary has the forms and the Colonel is making all the arrangements as we speak."

Rosemary must have heard her name because she came out of the kitchen waving forms in the air.

"Rosemary, can you please have a group of nurses call as many nonessential personnel as possible to help keep things running as smoothly as possible? I'm sure they would rather be doing something more productive than watching news reports that have nothing to tell us.

"Does anyone have any further questions?"

There was an uncomfortable silence in the room. Finally, hands started to go up.

"My name is Dr. Clarke and I'm head neurologist here. A group of us has already begun examining sleepers and it appears they are in a deep sleep like coma. We did an EEG on each and it appears their brain waves are abnormally high, higher even for someone not comatose. We are still studying the results, but our initial assessment is they appear to be in a deep REM state."

"The other phenomena we found fascinating is that after sleepers have an MRI that there is increased neural activity. It appears they are in the process of learning or forming new memories," said a doctor with the name Aster machine embroidered in blue on his long white lab coat.

"Forming new memories?" Janeen asked.

"Whatever they are dreaming about is causing them to learn—they aren't regular dreams."

"Dr. Clarke, Dr. Aster, that is interesting and I think it's something we should continue to evaluate. At last night's meeting a member of the CDC mentioned an unusual coma. I'll inquire more on that this afternoon. Thank you for being so proactive. If you could do a cross section of testing on sleepers, we can give your results to the CDC when they arrive tomorrow afternoon. You are welcome to sit in on the meeting. Perhaps your insights are something the CDC is unaware of."

"There are five of us who showed up today—myself, Dr. Aster, Dr. Hailey, Dr. Harmond, and Dr. Braco, and we will start as soon as the meeting is adjourned," Dr. Clarke said.

"I would like to discuss the results with you when you finish," Janeen said. "Now, on a final note, I want to say that we need each and every one of you here and I know the sacrifice some of you are making to do so. This is the largest catastrophe we've ever had to face and we can only survive it if we do it together. I know we have more questions than answers and that people are scared, but we need to put on a brave face for our sleepers and their families."

Heads nodded in agreement and Janeen believed she had just won them over. They'd stopped thinking about hospital politics and placed their priorities where they belonged, with the sleepers.

"Do we have any phlebotomists here today?"

Thirteen hands went up in the air.

"I want to assign two of you to the emergency room and I have another task for the rest of you. I would like to do a complete blood panel on all sleepers including a CMP and any other tests the neurologists might be able to use . . ."

A groan went through the crowd.

"I know, it's a time-consuming and massive job, but if you run fifty sleepers at a time it shouldn't make the task seem quite as daunting. I think it will be those of us working on the front lines who will find a solution to this dilemma."

Chapter 8

Washington, D.C., Saturday, April 15, 2017, 11:00 a.m.

LILLIAN Daniels joined a video conference call at NASA's Kennedy Space Center with President Mitchell, Dr. Lancaster, General Corbin Harrison, Dr. Walter Hickman of the CDC and his director of research, Dr. Colleen Giles, Allison Simmons, legal liaison for the sleepers of the occurrence, Steve Mathews, the president's press secretary, and Vice President Tempore Jared Smith.

"People, we have a lot to cover today and I hope you have some answers for me," the President said in his no-nonsense, take no prisoners voice. "Police and military personnel are struggling to locate all the sleepers, and in most cities across the nation are now searching every building looking for bodies, I've been considering the shortage of personnel in many areas who face this monumental task, and I have an idea. Steve, tonight you will announce in your news release that volunteers from local neighborhoods will be welcome to assist. Work with the General on assessing the areas where extra hands are needed and set up a meeting point for each area across the country. Hell, we'll bus people to wherever they're needed if we have to. We must find the sleepers as quickly as possible. General?"

"It would save us the time and effort we spend telling people to return to their homes. Some are just curious, but many people want to help, and I think it's an excellent idea. I'll work with Steve after our conference call on a detailed map and local meeting places. We'll meet up with volunteers at 0600 and stop when the sun starts to set."

"Alright, what's next on the agenda?"

"Mr. President, I would like to begin with my presentation first," Lilian Daniels said. "We are unable at this time to retrieve the astronaut. Many of our satellites are out and the one we need the most to bring the shuttle in is on the space station for repairs. Astronauts are doing a spacewalk now and are in the process of repairing it, but it will be another twenty-four hours before we can launch."

"Why are the satellites out?" the president asked.

"Mr. President, I'll try to explain this as simply as possible because it's a complicated topic and there are differences among scientists about whose theories are correct.

"On Tuesday our Solar Dynamics Observatory—this is an orbiting telescope around the sun—took images of sunspots. These are the areas that are black in the photos." She displayed a photo and gracefully traced her forefinger along a spattering of black spots on the broiling orange surface of the sun. "They are seven times the size of the Earth. The last time spots of this magnitude occurred in recorded history was in 1869, causing the largest geomagnetic storm in our historic era. A geomagnetic storm of this magnitude will short circuit satellites and disturb our communication systems. This storm measured thirty percent higher than the one in 1869. The problem with magnetic storms is we don't always have warning when they are going to occur. Normally we see increased activity building up on the surface of the sun, but that wasn't the case on Tuesday—they began to erupt without any warning. It takes forty-eight hours for us to feel the results of a magnetic storm."

Lilian displayed the iPad again, this time with a close-up image of the sun with the large sunspots magnified. "Now under normal circumstances, they post no immediate danger to Earth other than shooting streams of radiation outward from the sun in our direction. Thursday's occurrence was unprecedented. The 3X solar flares precipitated a geomagnetic storm here on Earth that disabled ninety percent of our satellites and is still affecting telephone reception."

President Mitchell looked stunned. "Wait a moment, you're telling me that what happened on the sun caused millions of people to collapse?"

"We can't say that definitively, but here is the interesting part. The solar flares erupted at 7:01 and continued every hour after that. For reasons we can't explain, NASA believes that these solar storms must be associated with the occurrence. Scientists look for causes, not coincidences, Mr. President, and the flare timeline pinpoints the progression of the occurrence in time zones around the world, exactly when people began to collapse in the same periodic progression. We can't give you the answers as to why, but our scientists are doing everything within our capability to find out."

"What about the satellites? When will they be in operation again?"

"Fifty percent of them have already reset and are operational, but the space station was hit harder than the rest. A cold boot isn't going to reset it. We need to repair the satellite from outside. Three astronauts are outside the space station right now, trying to repair the damage so we can launch a space shuttle to bring back the astronaut Colonel Richards who collapsed."

"First, do we have any additional theories that are viable?" the President asked brusquely. "And second, is there any way to continue treating Colonel Richards on the space station for any longer than it takes to restore the satellite? If the coma state seems benign and most patients simply need feeding, hydration, and vital signs checked, for the most part, as well as personal care—so far—can't this be accomplished on the station until the situation here is better understood?"

Lillian Daniels began speaking before Dr. Hickman could respond. "Under normal circumstances there is always a Doctor on board the shuttle, but we just brought one back and the next scheduled shuttle launch had the replacement physician. We have walked Colonel Fields through inserting an IV for fluids, but he was unable to incubate the patient. It is imperative we get Colonel Richards back to Earth."

Dr. Hickman cleared his throat before speaking. "To answer your first question Mr. President, we have been running tests nonstop since Thursday. We are sending a group of scientists to Boston Mass to duplicate those tests to see if we get the same results. Dr. Colleen Giles is in charge of this research team and I will let her explain."

"Thank you, Dr. Hickman. The first commonality that we saw in testing the victims is that they are all in a deep REM sleep, but as you know we can't wake them. We ran EEGs and their brain waves are higher than if they were awake. The section of the brain that appears most active is memory and learning. We are only at the initial testing phase and we are working on a test to try and wake one of them up," Dr. Giles said with conviction. "We believe these sleepers are aware of their surroundings, they have a high degree of consciousness. For some unexplainable reason they have not only entered a comatose state, but possibly an unprecedented or at least, previously unresearched, altered state, perhaps a hyperaware, enhanced dream state.

"Our scientists are in contact with Dr. Bethany Moore, a neurologist who has been testing this theory on animals. We need to try to turn on or stimulate the prefrontal cortex. In vegetative states this happens naturally after a period of time, the research has been unable to determine why some regained consciousness, and some didn't. By injecting dopamine or epinephrine, a neurotransmitter, early research shows that we can reawaken the dormant circuitry that is keeping them comatose. Dr. Jenkins is on her way to the CDC to work with scientists to determine the amount of dopamine we should insert. This is not a solution, Mr. President, it is a viable theory and one of the few that we have."

"For the non-scientists in the room, Dr. Jenkins, can you explain what dopamine is and what it does?" The president asked.

"It is a hormone, something that our bodies produce naturally, a neurotransmitter, a chemical released by nerve cells to communicate with other nerve cells . . . Mr. President, this is a type of coma we've never seen before. Normally we would call it a vegetative state except their brain waves and the REM phases rules that out. It is a state we just can't name at this point. The first of its kinds."

The President sat back in his chair and sighed heavily. "I want hourly reports on the progress and I want to know when you are going to begin the trials. Dr. Lancaster where are we are setting up facilities for the affected?"

"We have the facilities Mr. President; FEMA protocol and your executive order allowed us to use all stadiums and sports facilities as emergency medical facilities. The problem is the shortage of medical supplies. Manufacturers are running shifts 24/7, but progress is still slow. In many cases, we are using blenders to process food for tube feeding, but there are simple things like beds and even more essential medical equipment for testing that we can't gather medical data without. We also do not have the personnel to continue producing food by hand for the millions of people who are in need."

"I'll speak with medical supply companies personally. If we have to, we'll send in military personnel to assist their employees. General, where are we at on collecting sleepers?"

"Major looting is under control in most metropolitan areas at this point. Even so, I believe the six o'clock curfew should stay in effect for the foreseeable future. We need to keep a military presence in all cities to reinforce law enforcement agencies. Searching for and transporting sleepers and bodies has become time consuming. We are now going door to door and not everything we find is pleasant. Unfortunately, there are incidents of murder-suicide when panic overwhelmed some citizens during the first wave of the occurrence. Rumors are flying among fundamentalist Christians that the apocalypse is coming and while some are waiting for their predicted Rapture, others took the easy way out. We've also run across a pack of coyotes in Los Angeles that are feeding on sleepers left outdoors. We have every person at our resource on American streets and unless you want to reactivate the draft, Mr. President, we're at our limits as to what we can do."

"General, to maintain stability and the confidence of the American people, we need to find as many sleepers as possible. I think the volunteer program will give you the people you need, Americans are generous, take-charge people and want to be involved. We have to be an example to the world. In North Korea, our operatives have discovered that in the countryside, soldiers are digging deep ditches for the disposal of bodies and covering up these operations. They are broadcasting on television that these are victims of terrorism from the West. They don't have enough resources and facilities to care for sleepers of the occurrence; apparently, live sleepers are being eliminated by the millions. We have no idea what is happening in areas of the Middle East held by ISIS. Other countries are asking for our help and I've turned them down as we are struggling to provide resources for our own people. That's why we need to find answers quickly. We need to be proactive in discovering how to wake people up.

"Particular members of Congress have already expressed their opinion in press interviews that we are not doing all we can for their particular states. I want to put a stop to that," President Mitchell said forcefully.

"Dr. Giles, I need you to work with Kenneth to explain what you've just told us in a way that any average American can understand. I am also going to announce the volunteer search program in my news brief tonight, and I'm going to challenge the Senate and Congress to do their part and join search parties or volunteer for medical duties."

Kenneth cleared his throat to gain the President Mitchell's attention. "Mr. President, do you think we should discuss the unproven theory about the comas at this time?"

"People need to have faith in their government. Everyone needs something to hold onto and we're going to give them that."

Ms. Simmons raised her hand as if she were in school. "Mr. President, so much of what the mainstream media speculates about on television is terrifying. Don't you think we should counter this with positive reports on progress being made?"

"Ms. Simmons, you can take your film crews in tomorrow and tour Boston Mass—they are in full operation, and patient care assistants start their training tomorrow. They will soon house over five thousand sleepers and have reopened their emergency room. Colonel Forester is your contact and he will show you around. Other news agencies around the world are also airing news clips of the horrors that have taken place and I want to show the world that we are making progress."

President Mitchell placed his fingers together before him in a gesture of confidence. "You can contact me if you need me and if not, we will meet again tomorrow morning at the same time."

Chapter 9

THE noise in the sanctuary was vociferous and discourteous and Nathaniel Long looked upon his flock with disapproval. He understood their excitement and so after saying a silent prayer for patience, he thumped his Bible on the podium, silencing the deacons, the men's, women's, and youth Bible study groups, and the choir.

Taking his cue, Bob Jacobs stood before the group and chastised them.

"The evangelist is going to speak now and we need to pay attention. Tomorrow is the day we've been waiting for all our lives."

Although Nathaniel was technically their pastor, everyone referred to him as the evangelist. No one called him pastor to his face. They knew that he was anointed by God and paid him due respect as one of God's highest servants, the chosen one.

The room remained quiet as Nathaniel took a sip of water before speaking. He was wearing his baptismal robes tonight and no one seemed to have noticed, or if they did, they had kept their thoughts to themselves.

"I gather you here tonight because on Thursday we saw the first sign of the apocalypse. Tomorrow morning I will finally reveal to you what God has told me in my prayer closet, and you will know what you must do to follow his words. Time is short before the antichrist reveals himself and I must know you are prepared. I baptized each of you in this very sanctuary, but I must know you are pure of heart. We will take two hours to pray and meditate on God's word and while you do that, each of you must come to me and confess your deepest and darkest sins. Afterwards, I will baptize you once again in the name of the Lord and you will know that you are sanctified and worthy to carry out his word."

He had selected this group specifically because they were weak in the flesh and their sins an abomination to the Lord. They wanted God's forgiveness and they would do what he was going to call them to do because of that. There were gays, lesbians, child molesters, rapists, thieves, and all other namable sins in this room. He had prepared them for tomorrow without giving away too much. He had spent twenty years whetting their appetite for vengeance against Satan and his followers. He had never doubted that this day would come and that he would lead believers in one of the greatest wars against mankind.

Nathaniel bowed his head and led them in prayer before leaving the pulpit to hear their confessions. Tonight their baptisms would be different from what they had originally experienced. He had purchased three lambs and drained their blood into the baptismal. Tonight they would wash in the blood of the lamb.

Chapter 10

Burbank, California, Saturday, April 15, 2017, 5:00 p.m.

AFTER conferencing with all Boston tent cities, Janeen had left Forester as he explained what the military would do for them. The military had nearly completed construction of the tent cities in Boston and they had nearly filled all beds. Their biggest problem was that they didn't always have conventional beds or enough personnel to care for them. Janeen told them that she could spare two hundred nurses and fifty doctors. Forester suggested that they call in experienced nursing assistants, physician's assistants, respiratory therapists, and other medical tech applicants for interviews. They also had close to a hundred and fifty volunteers each who had submitted applications and could begin work immediately.

The emergency room had been open since 2:00 p.m., and Janeen wanted to check on their progress. When she entered, she was shocked that there was standing room only. The admissions registration clerk at the front desk looked frazzled and on the verge of tears. Janeen read her nametag, Sandy, and asked her to buzz her through the security doors.

A charge nurse at a station inside the ER looked relieved to see her striding toward a nursing station surrounded by improvised gurneys filled with patients. "Dr. Corbett, am I glad to see you. We've filled every single cubicle and gurney and everyone is running around like crazy. We've had a few heart attacks—family members or friends of sleepers—and we've sent them upstairs to the CICU unit for monitoring. Two need to be in the cath lab, but the cardiac doctors on duty are all down here."

Janeen looked up to see Rosemary and Laureen standing close behind her. She opened the door and let them in.

Rosemary looked flushed and took a deep breath before she spoke. "I was just looking for you. We've filled all available beds in the tent city—some beds are military cots or inflatables - and twenty some are simply beds made from blankets. I had to send the military transports and city emergency vehicles to other hospitals. I called each hospital to find out how many beds each still has open.

"We have a hundred experienced people with various medical qualifications hired and these will begin working tomorrow along with a hundred fifty volunteers. Half our day nurses said they would work through the night until the newbies start tomorrow. The new cafeteria night staff has arrived for orientation and will start their shifts at midnight. At least we can get something nutritious to eat around the clock."

"Rosemary, I'm going to take over for two cardiologists who have patients upstairs that need to go into the cath lab. Could you help out in here for a few hours? I'm desperate and that would be a life saver."

The ER door opened and Sandy stood against it to hold it open. "Dr. Corbett, I could really use help checking people in," she asked in a pleading tone. "With all the rush to get volunteers and extra medical personnel, they've forgotten to add admission clerks here in the ER. Admission clerks from upstairs will have to work some extra hours down here."

"Laureen, do you think you could help Sandy out for now? All you have to do is fill out basic information on the admission form for patients unable to fill these out themselves. We're not going to worry about insurance at this point. We just need names, addresses, medications they are on, and physical complaint. You'll hand them to Sandy so she can prioritize them and complete the data entry," Janeen said in a rush.

"I . . . I . . ."

Rosemary wrapped her arm around Laureen's waist and gave her a squeeze. "You can do it, Laureen, I know you can, and we really need your help."

"Okay," Laureen said, still clutching her Bible. She went to stand next to Sandy who began to explain the forms.

Janeen pressed the intercom button and paged two cardiologists, Dr. Hailey and Dr. Clarke to the front desk. When they arrived, she could see by the looks on their frazzled faces that they were exhausted.

"I know you're tired but we have patients up in CICU. I'll take over your duties here."

"Bed two in bay ten needs stiches. He was in a car crash on Thursday," Dr. Morse said. He then turned around and rapidly walked towards the elevators.

"I think bed one in bay five has a minor concussion, but there's a line of about twenty people in triage ahead of him. I suggest sending him home with instructions to stay awake or to have someone keep an eye on him and give him a time to return," Dr. Hailey said.

"I'll take care of them. Rosemary, go see the concussion patient and I'll take care of the stitches."

Janeen hurried to bay ten and grabbed a pair of latex gloves on her way in.

"We've been waiting for two hours to be seen," said a young woman severely, while holding a toddler on her lap. "We were in a car crash and I tried to butterfly the wound, but it keeps opening."

The boy sitting on his mother's lap was sucking his thumb and appeared to be around three.

Janeen grabbed a lollipop out of her hospital gown (she carried them wherever she went) and smiled at the child. "Here you are. Can you tell me your name?"

The little boy shook his head no.

"His name is Henry and the cut is above his knee," the mother said.

Janeen smiled and asked her name.

She began to cry. "It's Karen. I don't mean to be nasty—I've just been worried sick. To make things worse, my husband Jeff hasn't come home. I think he's a victim of the occurrence and I don't know how to find him."

"The City of Boston is working on a website and to display on local television stations the names and photos of those who've been picked up. It probably won't happen for a day or two, but I wouldn't be worried. The military is searching for everyone—they are in good hands," Janeen exaggerated. "Let me look at Henry's leg."

Janeen pulled the toddler's jeans leg up and looked at the small, jagged cut. "He only needs about eight stitches. If you will hold him tightly so that I can numb the area, this shouldn't take long."

When Janeen was finished, she handed Henry another lollipop and finally got a smile out of him. When they left the room, she quickly changed the sheets for the next patient.

She returned to the nurses' station and flipped through the list of patients. She then called out five names. "If you will all follow me, we'll get you taken care of."

She led them all into the same room that Henry had used. Four out of the five displayed surprised expressions. "I know this is unorthodox, but we are out of beds and short on doctors and space. According to your paperwork, you all need stitches, so I'll take you one by one. Mr. Swartz, you're up first."

Janeen examined the wound on the middle-aged man's forehead and decided that a butterfly would do the trick. He thanked her graciously after her treatment and left the room.

The next four patients needed stitches, nothing life threatening, and Janeen had them all finished within an hour. She returned to the nurses' station, where there was less hubbub than the hour before, and then went outside to the admissions desk and noted that the waiting area wasn't quite as full.

"Rosemary is an angel," Sandy said. "She went through the list and sent half of them home; most just had bumps and bruises from the pileup on the interstate. We did have one woman in labor and she is up in obstetrics. Thank goodness her husband is with her because she is terrified that something will be wrong with the baby."

"I'm going to head up there now—it looks like everything is under control here."

"Yes, thirty doctors and nurses are taking their dinner break and believe me, they deserve it. She turned to Laureen. And our volunteer here made my job so much easier."

Laureen beamed for the first time since Janeen had met her. "Thank you, Sandy—you make sure you get something to eat as well. If Laureen has time, she can stay here while you go to the cafeteria."

Janeen decided to take the stairs to the ninth floor and went she hit the second floor landing she found a little girl curled up into a ball, crying.

Janeen approached the girl quietly and squatted beside her. "Hello, little one. My name is Dr. Corbett and I work here at the hospital. Can I help you find your mommy or daddy?"

The girl looked up, her dirty face stained with tear tracks. "I don't know where my mommy is. She went to work and left me with Sarah, she's my babysitter. Today Sarah brought me here and said my mommy was gone and she wasn't going to babysit me forever. I want my mommy," the little girl sobbed.

"Come here, honey, I'm going to help you. What's your name?"

"Michelle, but mommy calls me Shelly. Can you find my mommy?"

"It might take us awhile, but I'm sure we can find her. How old are you, Shelley?"

"I'm five and I'm in kindergarten. My teacher is Miss Langstrom—maybe she knows where my mommy went."

"Come on with me and we'll see if we can find her. What school do you attend, Shelley?"

"Eliot Elementary School. I didn't go to school the other day cause I had a cold, but I feel better now."

Janeen took Shelley's hand and entered the second floor. A security guard stood near the door. "I need you to do something for me. Can you contact Eliot Elementary School and see if there is a woman . . . what's you mommy's first and last name Shelley?"

"Her name is Bonnie Smith."

"Can you contact the Red Cross there and ask to speak to a Bonnie Smith? If she's there let her know her daughter is safe and we will bring her to the school. Colonel Forester will arrange it. If you don't find her, just page me and I'll come and get Shelley."

"Shelley, I'm going to leave you with this nice man and we're going to see if we can find your mommy."

Janeen took out a lollipop and the little girl smiled brightly. "Thank you, Doctor," she said with a slight lisp.

It had been a long day and Janeen decided to take the elevator after all. When she reached the obstetrics floor, the entire corridor was crowded with people. She made her way through the crowd toward the ward door. When she looked up, Rosemary stood there holding the door open.

"In times of trouble, Doc you need a miracle. This might be just what we need."

A few seconds later, the cry of a newborn baby echoed from a delivery suite and the crowd whooped and hollered in celebration.

Janeen entered to see a smiling man and a young woman holding their baby for the first time. The two nurses and the obstetrician were smiling through their tears.

"The baby is perfectly healthy and she was anxious to make an entrance. I'm about to perform a C-section on my other patient—let's hope that story has a happy ending too."

Chapter 11

Boston Mass, Saturday, April 15, 2017, 8:00 p.m.

JANEEN had just finished her call with Dr. Lancaster and had learned of the trials that they planned to conduct on eight of the sleepers at Boston Mass. He also informed her that the CDC wanted to set up an additional operations center in Boston. She explained what her neurologists had discovered and it coincided with Dr. Gregg's findings.

"The theory, using dopamine to stimulate their cerebral cortex, behind awakening the sleepers seems valid, the cause seems farfetched," Janeen said.

"I originally agreed with you, but as doctors, we have to look at cause and effect of solar activity. Solar flares affect the Earth's ionosphere and disrupt GPS and radio transmissions, and coronal mass ejections cause more serious effects, such as knocking out satellites and electrical grids, but neither has ever been linked to human health until now.

"Lillian Daniels, the head of NASA, is convinced that the correlation between the occurrence and the recent solar activity is not a coincidence and after our conference call, I did a bit of research. The electromagnetic storm that happened in 1869 didn't have any effect on people, at least none that were recorded. She is correct that this one was 30 percent worse though.

"However, although the storm in 1869 didn't have any recorded physical effects on people, scientists have watched them closely since that time. They have proven that these storms affect people's behavior. Emergency rooms statistics show consistent observed increases in injuries resulting from violence during an electromagnetic storm. There is also a list of physical effects from the storms, which Columbia University has documented. Sleep patterns are disturbed, nervousness, irritability, hot flashes, headaches, nausea, heart palpitations, as well as heart attacks, mood swings, and erratic behavior. Increased violence seems to be at the top of the list and if she is correct, it might explain what we are seeing now. Not all people who we've arrested are known criminals or gang members. There are professionals with good incomes and families arrested for violence in the streets. Police statistics show that there is an increase of domestic violence calls. If her theory is correct, we can't predict when this could happen again," Dr. Lancaster explained.

Janeen was quiet for a moment fascinated by the science. "How do solar storms affect sleep?"

"I found this element fascinating," Dr. Lancaster said. "Electromagnetic activity affects the pineal gland in our brain. It causes it to produce excess melatonin, which is the brain's mechanism that helps us sleep. Excess melatonin affects our circadian rhythm, in other words our biological clock. During a solar storm, research was done on sleeping and they discovered that many people wake up between 1:00 a.m. to 2:00 a.m. and are unable to fall back to sleep."

"If these statistics are correct, what would we do when the next storm hits?" Janeen asked.

"We have a forty-eight hour window from the time the storm starts on the sun until it reaches us here on Earth. We could declare martial law and restrict everyone to their homes, but if it did cause these comas then there is nothing we could do to prevent it from happening again."

"The question still remains as to why only these particular people fell into a coma," Janeen said.

"That is something that researchers will focus on once we get the sleepers back on their feet. We've shared our theory with scientists around the globe, and they are awaiting the results of our testing. Right now, it's the only theory we've come up with."

"Would you mind sending me the data you discovered, I'd like to first review it and then share it with our Doctors here?

"How is it going on the West Coast?" Janeen asked.

"I've found enough facilities; I just don't have the personnel. We might have to send sleepers to smaller communities if I can't convince the doctors and nurses to relocate temporarily. We have the Staples Center and the Orange Bowl, but it seems there's a church out here who wanted to rent them for the day tomorrow. Can you imagine a church wanting to use a designated public shelter in the midst of a crisis?"

"Nothing surprises me," Janeen responded. "Are you going to be here tomorrow when the CDC arrives?"

"No, I still have business in the West. I've given them your name and told them you'll help set them up. I'm going to run so I can listen to the President, so I'll talk with you tomorrow."

"Before you go, there is something I haven't mentioned because we just discovered it tonight. The patient's irises are all turning gold. Although jaundice occurs in the whites of the eyes, we are going to run the test as a precaution. We are also testing for hepatitis. We've also noted that those that are not turning gold have a white film over the pupil, similar to cataracts, although the optometrist we have on staff has ruled that out."

"Interesting," Dr. Lancaster responded. "I'm going to check with other tent cities to see if they are noticing this phenomenon."

* * *

The President had a speech scheduled at 9:00 p.m. and Janeen made the announcement over the loudspeaker so that people would be able to watch it. Spirits were high after the birth earlier and Janeen thought that the President's new information would raise them even higher.

She stood with Rosemary and Laureen outside the obstetrics surgical suite to wait for a report from Dr. Caddell. He had originally scheduled Judith Galloway for a C-section the following day, but under the circumstances, he felt it imperative to remove the child as soon as possible. The sonogram had showed no movement and the heartbeat was faint.

The other women's babies all seemed active, but the obstetrician had decided that those who had reached thirty-six weeks would undergo C-sections the next day as well.

The door slammed open and a doctor Janeen didn't recognize threw his surgical gown in the bin and said "Fuck" as he pushed them aside. A few minutes later Dr. Caddell walked out pulling off his surgical gown. Janeen could tell by the look on his face that the news wasn't good.

"The baby was stillborn. The mother is fine, however. I knew from the sonogram that things weren't good. I should have tried to perform the surgery then."

"You can't blame yourself, Dr. Caddell. You were running tests on all thirty-nine women today and you did bring one healthy child into the world."

"I know . . . I know. I just hate losing one. We're starting the C-sections tomorrow morning at 6:00 a.m. We have no idea what this coma does to a fetus or a baby close to the due date and we want to give them all a fighting chance. Other than you three and the other obstetricians, we are going to keep this quiet. People's spirits were so high tonight and there is a crowd standing by the neonatal unit making faces and cooing at the baby. Something about newborn infants can soften the hardest heart."

"How many babies and toddlers do we have that are sleepers from the occurrence?"

"Twenty-four. Ages six weeks to three years. Anyone over a year old is on floor seven, the pediatric unit. We brought in additional cribs for the seventh floor. So far they all seem healthy and we have a group of pediatricians monitoring them."

"I wanted to let you know that the president is speaking at 9:00 p.m. and his press secretary is speaking now."

"I'll go watch it in the doctor's lounge. Thanks for letting me know."

Janeen watched the surgeon walk away; his slouched shoulders indicated he felt defeated and was carrying a burden.

She knew exactly how he felt, she had lost a few patients herself in the ER, and there was nothing anyone could say that would make it any better. Condolences felt like mere platitudes and tended to make her feel worse. Maybe she'd blown it and should have let him do the talking while she patted him on the back in sympathy. Sometimes people didn't need comforting, they just needed to have someone listen.

"Let's go down to the nurse's station and listen to President Mitchell's speech," Rosemary said quietly.

Janeen was paged over the loudspeaker and she rushed down to the nurse's station to pick up her call.

A harried-looking young nurse handed her a telephone receiver. "Dr. Corbett here," she said, out of breath.

"Janeen, it's Forester. I have some good news for you. The little girl you had Private Wilson take, well, we found her mother. She was at the school in the Red Cross shelter. The babysitter was too far away to get through all the checkpoints and she didn't have a car and the phones weren't working."

"Oh thank you. I could use some good news right about now."

"Why, what's going on?"

"The mother they performed the C-section on—the baby was still-born."

Forester sighed heavily. "Oh shit, that will definitely lower morale."

"We're keeping it quiet until we start the other C-sections tomorrow. Right now, everyone is on a high. They even have a baby name pool going. I don't want to burst their bubble.

"How about you, did you find enough bedding?"

"Well, we filled all twenty-five Boston hospitals and that's something else I needed to talk to you about. My soldiers volunteered to give up their three tents that they are using for temporary barracks so I put the rest of the sleepers there. I know we're short on personnel, but until we get Gillette Stadium set up, I didn't know what else to do. We still have twenty trucks full of victims, approximately two hundred sleepers, that we picked up today and since the medical personnel isn't due to start working until tomorrow at the stadium do you think you could pull your nurses to get their feeding tubes started?" Forester asked.

"I'll have to rescind my offer of doctors and nurses with the new amount of sleepers we have to take care of. I'll have them start working on sleepers in the trucks and then the tents. Can you get your guards to set up lights in the trucks so we can see to work? Many will need feeding before morning."

"I'm on it now, Janeen, thanks."

Janeen connected to the speaker to announce her requests. She asked the doctors to work alongside the nurses to speed the work. "I know you've all had a long day and you're exhausted, but some of these victims haven't had food since Thursday. Some may need medical attention. When the President's speech is over, if you could meet me by Tent 8, we can get started. I'll have military personnel grab boxes of supplies for us. I want each and every one of you to know how proud I am to be working with you."

Chapter 12

"MY fellow Americans, and to those who are listening outside the United States of America, good evening. We have made some great strides in progress today and that is what I want to share with you tonight.

"First, we have located enough facilities to house all the sleepers of Thursday's occurrence. These are being set up as we speak. Our military is working 24/7 to provide beds, bedding, and to deliver other necessary supplies needed to care for these people. On the East Coast, many hospitals have reopened their emergency rooms to the public as well as caring for sleepers of the occurrence. Boston Mass, where the occurrence first manifested itself, is housing over six thousand people and their emergency room is accepting any emergency. On an even brighter note, I'm told that a perfectly healthy child was born this evening at the hospital."

The President waited for the press applause to die down.

"Scientists at the CDC and across the globe are looking for a cause for the collapse and subsequent comatose state of last Thursday's sleepers. This is a coma that the medical community has never seen or classified before, but their work is progressing. Tomorrow, eight random victims will receive an experimental treatment to see if we can wake them from their sleep-like coma. We are in the early phase of diagnosing and treating these people, but progress is being made.

"On another bright note, the Space Station satellite repairs are now complete and tomorrow a launch is set at 6:30 a.m. to retrieve Colonel Richards, our brave astronaut who, like so many other Americans, fell victim to the occurrence.

"Medical research takes time. We hope to prevent this from ever happening again as well as pinpointing the cause. So many families are separated tonight and their suffering is heartfelt. We must all exert a profound level of patience as we wait for confirmed information—it is not in our best interest to indulge in wild speculation or to create unfounded rumors. We must wait until we have scientific proof as to what occurred and I know this wait is a difficult thing to ask of you. We must rely on our faith to see us through in our time of need.

"A database of both unidentified and identified sleepers will be available starting on Monday morning through the US Department of Health and Human Services at hhs.gov. Tune into channel three for instructions on which channel to turn to as we have divided them alphabetically. It will not be a fast system, but we have data entry clerks and volunteers working around the clock. The majority of communications satellites are now working, but the numbers of people searching the Internet may slow it down considerably, so the database will also be posted at C-SPAN 3 as well as on local community networks. You'll find a list of local channels available at C-SPAN 3. I'm told there are also physical "bulletin boards" springing up in cities around the country, and people are posting pictures of their missing loved ones at these locations. If you have had contact with any missing persons or any victim you know whose family may not be aware of their condition, there will also be 800 numbers available to report these contacts. Law enforcement agencies around the country are doing everything possible to assist with the flow of information. You may call any non-emergency number at any law enforcement agency to seek information about missing family members.

"Martial law will continue to be in effect for the foreseeable future. Millions of people have fallen victim and though disturbances in the streets are mostly under control, a six o'clock curfew will continue to remain in force, except for necessary medical, law enforcement, or military personnel.

"There are businesses with important jobs that must reopen soon, if they're not already; food processing plants, medical equipment and supply manufacturers and the corresponding wholesale and retail businesses such as grocery stores, pharmacies, and medical supply outlets. We will allow employees in essential businesses to start returning to work on Tuesday, April 18, 2017. Wall Street and banks will remain closed until further notice. Please have ID with you as you go through checkpoints. Traffic will be slow because of these necessary checks and you should leave a sufficient time window if you have to travel on the interstate.

"I want to congratulate the American people for their patience and stamina and for their admirable responses to this crisis. Yes, we've had rioting and looting, but we have many more people who are volunteering their time to help care for the sleepers of this catastrophe. Neighbors are helping neighbors, and volunteers of every class, creed, culture, and economic status have joined our military and law enforcement agencies in their door-to-door search for sleepers. We have shown our strength in this time of need and Americans have made me weep with their generosity. My thoughts are with each and every one of you, at home and abroad, and I can assure you that we will continue to keep you informed. God Bless America—and the world. Goodnight."

Chapter 13

THE hospital staff had been hard at work since Janeen's announcement at 9:30 p.m. The first shift of nurses had stayed and the second shift had arrived. She had sent seventy-five of the obstetricians and surgical nurses to sleep at home or in the hospital, because all had surgery in the morning. Surprisingly enough, the task of inserting feeding tubes and catheters in the newest sleepers still held in trucks had been finished. These sleepers were left wearing their own clothing because the nights were still cool. They had just started care in the tents and this would take longer as they were diapering and changing sleepers from their clothes into hospital gowns. If they found identification, they taped it to the end of the bed. Laureen had been helpful as she had taken digital photos of the sleepers and these would go to Forester in the morning to send to the appropriate people.

Forester had his personnel call all volunteers on the list and asked them to come in. A hundred and three people showed up and many wept when they saw all the sleepers.

As Janeen worked, she realized no one ever referred to these people as patients, but always, from the beginning as sleepers. Perhaps it made it easier to deal with the situation emotionally. As a doctor, she had learned to put her emotions aside and attend to her job of treating bodies. It wasn't as easy as they taught you in school. A perfect example was the stillborn baby. Both obstetricians had reacted emotionally, and you could see the pain on their faces.

President Mitchell's speech earlier had lifted the spirits of her staff. They all cheered when he mentioned Boston Mass and their pride showed clearly on their faces. This translated to a boost of energy and tonight's work seemed to be happening at breakneck speed.

Rosemary had just finished inserting a catheter on one man and Janeen had finished the feeding tube when she stopped and put a hand on Rosemary's shoulder.

"You need to go and get some rest Rosemary. We've got this covered now—even some of the volunteers are able to insert catheters. Go spend some time with your husband and then get some sleep."

"I would argue with you under normal circumstances, but we ended up with four hundred medical assistant applications and two hundred are showing up at 8:00 a.m. If we end up not needing all of them, we can send them to the stadium or one of the other hospitals."

"I don't know what I would have done without you today, Rosemary," Janeen said with a deep breath.

"It's my job," Rosemary said with a weary smile. "Talking about sleep—you have one hell of a day tomorrow with the CDC coming and you haven't even yet picked out the sleepers you think they should test their theory on."

"I'll do that when they get here. They'll want a cross section of people, of course. I promise to be in bed by 2:00. Three hours will do me and I promise to take that power nap sometime tomorrow. Why don't you take Laureen with you and get her a bed in the staff quarters?"

Janeen had no intention of going to bed; she would stay until as many sleepers as possible had received the care they needed. The longer the night wore on, the faster everyone seemed to work, Finally, at 4:30 a.m. the majority of sleepers had what they needed. Janeen sent the first shift home and asked volunteers if they could come back tomorrow at 09:00. Now that everyone had a feeding tube, IV, and catheter bag, it was time to start at the beginning and feed each sleeper, change their diapers, empty the catheter bag, and reposition them. Janeen suggested they work in teams of two. One hundred and fifty experienced nurses could get five sleepers taken care of in ten minutes working in pairs. Janeen asked who the head nurse was and ten hands went up.

"I'm going to leave it to you ten to decide how to divide up the tents. I'm not even sure when each sleeper last had care."

A nurse with a nametag reading Steve raised his hand. "Rosemary left nursing instructions at the front desk. We have everything under control. You go grab some coffee and put your feet up for a bit," he said with authority.

"I'm not going to argue," Janeen said with a wan smile.

All the volunteers, patient care assistants, nurses, and technicians moved back to Tents 1 and 2 and Janeen remained in Tent 11 after they left. It was so silent in here because there were no EKG machines. The quiet gave her an eerie feeling and she felt goosebumps running up her arms. She was covering up one of the sleepers with a blanket and heard a noise. She looked up to see three volunteers entering the tent from the other side. They were each holding a butcher knife. Janeen's first thought was where were the guards that were supposed to be guarding the entrance? She walked to the center isle and screamed at the top of her lungs for a guard. The three men ignored her and they each stood by a set of bunk beds and proceeded to cut the sleepers throats. She had no weapons to protect them and felt tears sliding down her cheeks. Suddenly, from the other end of the tent, she saw guards running towards her with their weapons drawn. They entered the tent and a guard she recognized from earlier today shouted, "Halt".

The three men looked up from what they were doing and they each sneered.

"We are doing the Lord's work. You have no power over us," said the largest of the men.

"If you don't drop your knives, we will shoot you," said the guard.

Two of the men raised their hands in the air and dropped their knives to the ground. The largest man turned and starred at Janeen. He held his knife above his head and began to run towards her.

Janeen told her feet to run, but they refused to obey her and she remained frozen in place.

The man's eyes were wide and he had a look of triumph on his face.

Suddenly, the tent was filled with gunfire and Janeen finally moved. She dropped to the ground and covered her ears to block out the sound that filled the tent.

The man's face changed and he opened his mouth in the shape of an O. Janeen watched as a trickle of blood ran from his mouth to his chin and he fell forward, the knife still grasped tightly in his hand.

The gunfire stopped, but Janeen was unable to move, the shock of what she had just witnessed kept her glued to the ground.

Janeen felt an arm around her and she looked up to see Dr. Clark's concerned face.

"Here, let me help you up," he said softly. "Are you hurt?"

"No, I'm alright Dr. Clark," she said standing up.

"Call me Carl."

"We need to check on the sleepers, I think they killed three of them."

One of the Doctors, she didn't recognize, leaned over the man who the guards had shot and proclaimed him dead.

"Where the hell were you," Janeen shouted at the guard. "There is supposed to be security here."

"I'm sorry ma'am. We were moving all the trucks filled with sleepers and Colonel Forester hadn't assigned anyone to the three additional tents."

Janeen was too furious to speak and she followed Carl to check on the sleepers. They had killed five of them and she felt tears filling her eyes.

"You can give your condolences to the families of these sleepers. Fuck," she screamed.

By now, the tent had started filling up with personnel.

"We need six gurneys. I need orderlies to move these bodies to the morgue," Janeen said. "Everybody go back to work, there is nothing more to see here."

Janeen turned to the guard whose nametag read Taylor. "Taylor, I want extra guards posted on these three tents. If you have a problem with that, I'll be glad to talk to Colonel Forester myself."

"No ma'am, I'll see to it now," he said turning red.

Guards surrounded the two other killers and began to push them forward out of the tent. As people began to return to their duties, Carl walked over and put his hand on her shoulder. "Are you sure you're alright?"

"I'm just really pissed off right now. These religious fanatics are really becoming a problem and we need more protection. I'm going to call Colonel Forester in the morning and update him. The coma is bad enough, but now we have worry about their safety."

Carl leaned forward and gently wiped away her tears with his thumbs. "This isn't your fault Janeen."

"It's my responsibility to keep them safe until we can wake them up from their comas," Janeen said trying to pull herself together.

"You can only do so much and this is Forester's screw-up, not yours."

"I appreciate your concern Carl. I'm just overly tired and a bit in shock. They came in and there was nothing I could do to protect the sleepers. I think I just need some time to compose myself. If you'll excuse me, I'm going to go get cleaned up."

"I'm here if you need to talk," Carl said as Janeen turned away.

On her way back to the doctor's lounge, Janeen decided to stop by the cafeteria. As promised, workers were busy in the kitchen.

Ethel was standing by the stove and turned around to greet her. "Dr. Corbett, Rosemary said you might be coming back here and that you haven't eaten all day. I've made you Texas French toast, a half dozen of those sausages you love, and I just made a fresh pot of coffee.

"Are you okay, you look a bit flustered?"

Janeen knew it wouldn't be long before Ethel heard what had happened to the rumor mill, but she just didn't have the energy to share what had happened. "Just tired Ethel, but after what I've been through tonight I could use a stiff drink, but I guess coffee will have to do. You know Ethel, you are my angel. I'm starving. If you wouldn't mind, I'll pull up a chair here in the kitchen while I eat and keep you company."

"Of course. You are always welcome, Doc," Ethel said with a smile.

Janeen dug into her meal and realized how hungry she was. The sausages were cooked to perfection and it tickled her that Ethel remembered that Texas French toast was her favorite.

"How is the kitchen going now that you're back?"

Ethel looked up from stirring a large pot of oatmeal and turned around to give Jannen a broad grin. "We'll have to be creative if we don't get a delivery in the next few days, but no one will go hungry. We're running two shifts and everyone is glad to be back here. It's not healthy sitting home and watching new reports all day. A few of the staff have family here, and Millie is one of the sleepers. I don't know if you remember her, she was always the quiet one."

"I'm so sorry, Ethel. Tell me where she's at and I'll give her a physical today."

"Thanks Doc, but one of the head nurses already checked her. Her medical records were here so she won't go without her diabetes and high blood pressure meds."

"That's a relief. I'm worried about sleepers who have been without their meds since Thursday," Janeen said.

"Such a mess. I think everyone is still in shock. Seems like something you'd read about in some sci-fi novel. I just hope we get some answers soon. I watched President Mitchell tonight and the good news he shared. We're all praying that this experimental treatment works."

Janeen finished her breakfast, and gave Ethel a big hug. "Thank you Ethel. I really needed that."

"Don't miss lunch—I'm making lasagna. Rosemary had everything laid and out for us, and I'll keep a plate warm for you."

Janeen went to the doctor's staff lounge, grabbed a clean set of scrubs, and opened her locker to get her shampoo and grab a fresh towel. When she entered the shower room, she heard the shower nearest the door running and went to the opposite end. She turned the shower on its hottest setting and leaned her hands against the wall to allow the water to pummel her shoulders. The hot water soothed her stiff muscles and she found herself crying over the deaths of the sleepers. She finally cried herself out, wiped her nose off with the back of her hand, and grabbed a bar of soap. After washing and conditioning her hair, she slipped a towel around herself and stepped out. When she entered the changing room, she saw Dr. Caddell drying off his hair.

"Morning, Dr. Caddell."

"Damn, you scared me, Dr. Corbett. What in the world are you doing up so early after your long night?"

"I haven't been to bed yet and I was just about to come find you and ask if I could sit in on your first C-section. By the way, call me Janeen."

"I'm Dan. Of course you can. We actually have two surgical units running at the same time. We want those babies out as soon as possible."

"I can understand your urgency. Do we have enough room for twenty babies?"

"Yes, the communications officer arranged for the delivery of basinets yesterday and if we have to, we'll double them up. Well, time to scrub up. It's already near six."

"I'm going to dry my hair and I'll be right with you."

After Dan left, Janeen dried her hair quickly and slipped into her scrubs. She looked in the mirror, thought about makeup, and slammed her locker door shut. "Fuck it, it's the end of the world," she said, wrinkling her nose up at herself.

After scrubbing up, she snuck into the surgical suite just as Dan made his cut. He worked rapidly and Janeen found herself impressed. Soon the first cry of a newborn baby broke the silence.

"It's a boy," Dan said with a smile.

Janeen recognized Dr. Allen, a pediatrician, as he took the baby from Dan.

Dan instructed the other surgeon to close and went to stand beside the baby.

"Apgar score of nine. He's seven pounds, eight ounces, and 21 1/2 inches long. Lungs are clear, vitals are strong, eyes appear normal. Muscle tone is excellent. And he's a screamer. I'd say that you have a perfectly healthy boy here."

"Yes," shouted Dan. "Hurry up Henry, get her closed up so we can get the next one in here."

Janeen heard a shout from the other surgical suite and then the doors flew open.

"Six pounds, three ounces, and 19 inches long. She's perfect," Dr. Phillips said with a shout.

Dan smiled broadly. "Two down and eighteen to go."

"Congratulations, Doctors. Now how many are at the thirty-six week mark?" Colleen, a surgical nurse, asked.

"Twenty. We'll decide tomorrow on a case-by-case basis the other nineteen mothers. It will depend on how far along they are and the risk to the baby, if we should perform any additional C-sections," Dan said.

"Well, I'm glad to be here for the first one. Thanks for letting me sit in."

Dan winked at her. "Anytime."

When Janeen left the surgical suite, she wondered if Dan had just been enthusiastic after the baby's birth, or if he was flirting with her. She hadn't dated in so long that she could barely remember all the signals.

She had to admit that he was definitely her type. Sandy blond hair, gray eyes, over six feet tall, about 170 pounds, and he looked like a runner. Maybe when this was all over she would ask if he wanted to go for a run with her. First, she needed to talk to Rosemary and get the gossip on him.

Chapter 14

JANEEN had reserved the auditorium for her meeting with the CDC and had tables and whiteboards brought in for their use. She had also called the neurologists—Director Dr. Clarke, Dr. Aster, Dr. Hailey, Dr. Harmond, and Dr. Braco. She wanted to give them a heads-up before the CDC arrived.

Her first call this morning was the lab techs who took tests with the MRI, CAT scan, and EEG machines to make sure they were on duty. A little groggy, all said they would be in at 7:00 a.m.

"Good morning, Doctors, thank you for being here so early. The CDC is due here at 1:00 p.m. and I wanted to let you know what they discovered. You should pat yourselves on the back because they came back with the same theory and results you were working on.

"The first thing they noticed was the commonality that you saw in the sleepers. They were in REM states and their EEGs show that their brain waves were higher than if they were awake."

"I knew it," Dr. Clarke shouted out. "They are in a coma, one similar to a dream state, but a coma nonetheless."

"Let me guess," Dr. Aster said with a smile. "They are going to try and awaken them with dopamine or epinephrine to jumpstart the prefrontal cortex."

"My biggest concern," Dr. Clarke replied, "is that the sleepers would have to remain on the drug for life. There just isn't enough research on comas and so many unanswered questions and variables."

Janeen nodded her head in understanding. "I'm sure you'll be discussing many theories today and Dr. Bethany Moore, who devised the current theory of awaking the sleepers, will be here today as well. This has been her area of research for some time and I'm sure that you'll find some answers from such a distinguished group of neurologists. Of course, I don't need to remind you, that as we've learned, in science progress is normally one step ahead and two back, so don't get frustrated. We have too many people depending on us.

"Now, what did I did call to ask you? Oh, would you like to work with them in a consulting function? I'm sure they would appreciate the input. What do you say?"

"Are you kidding?" Dr. Clarke said. "This is a neurologist's dream. The fact we're thinking along the same scientific lines as the CDC is amazing."

"You can help them with a cross section of patients and work with them on anything else they need. I'll only be here for a short time, but as you know, my schedule is more than a bit overloaded," Janeen said with a laugh.

"Dr. Corbett, thank you so much for including us in this work toward a cure. We're going to need to move the machinery in here since we are going to use the auditorium to perform the experiments so we'll get to it," Dr. Clarke said as he rubbed his hands together in anticipation.

"I would like them to see the patient's brains that we did a brain scan on yesterday; we have one who seems like a perfect candidate because the coma doesn't appear as extreme as the others.

"We know how busy you are so we'll be waiting for you at 1:00 p.m. when the CDC guests arrive."

"We've agreed to give them a tour of tent city, so I suggest you wait here for us. Perhaps one of you could get a cafeteria worker to bring us a few carafes of coffee, juice, and perhaps a plate or two of cookies and a plate of fresh fruit, but only if they have sufficient supplies."

"I'll take care of that," Dr. Aster said.

"Wonderful, I shall see you all this afternoon."

Chapter 15

THE sanctuary was full at Los Angeles Outreach and Gospel Church and the choir had them singing and dancing in the isles. The Holy Spirit had made Itself known by all the speaking in tongues and people became so possessed by His spirit that they fell to the floor. The band played so loud that it didn't even need the speaker equipment. God's presence hung in the air and they felt purified when they inhaled His essence.

On cue, the singers and band quit playing and Nathaniel Long went to stand at the pulpit. Holding his Bible high in the air, he shouted. "Praise Jesus."

The crowed joined him and still he cried out "Praise Jesus."

He motioned for the crowds to sit and the tense silence in the sanctuary was palatable to Nathaniel Long.

"Welcome members and welcome to those at home who could not be with us today. Wherever we are, the Lord is with us all on this monumental day and his words will be spoken and shared with those who have not yet turned their lives over to him.

"Today's service is going to be unlike any you have ever experienced. We will not take an offering today because we are going to be too busy listening to God's word.

"We won't be offering communion today because we are going to sustain ourselves on the Holy Book. When you leave here today, your hearts and minds will take the Father, Son, and Holy Ghost with you. The time that we have waited for is finally here."

"Praise God," someone shouted out.

"Praise God indeed, brother. Can I get an amen?" Nathaniel shouted.

The sanctuary roof lifted from the shouting inside and outside the building.

Nathaniel smiled at the response and began his service. "In Revelations Chapter 5, John is worried about who is worthy to open the scroll and elders chastised him.

> *"Stop crying and look! The one called both the Lion from the Tribe of Judah and King David's great Descendant has won the victory of the one to break its seal."*

"Revelations 5:9 gives us the answer in a song.

> *"You are worthy to receive the scroll and open its seals,*
> *Because you were killed*
> *And with your own blood*
> *You bought for God*
> *People from every tribe, language, nation, and race.*
> *You let them become kings and serve God as priests,*
>   *and they will rule on earth."*

The sanctuary remained quiet until Nathaniel raised his bible into the air.

"Who was the lamb that died for our sins? The Son of God!"

The congregation began to shout out "The Son of God" over and over again and he let it go on for five minutes before lowering his hands for quiet.

"You may be asking yourselves why is our evangelist talking about the breaking of the seal, because, my fellow brethren and sisters, the seal has been broken, and God's will be done. For those of you who believe that last Thursday's occurrence was just another strange coincidence, I am here to tell you that Jesus Christ is alive and well and it will not be long before He walks among us.

"God has spoken to me and told me that today you must hear the truth of His word and go forth and follow His commandments. They are difficult tasks we must perform, but we must remember who we are dealing with. Who are we dealing with?"

"Satan," shouted the congregation.

"That is right," Nathaniel shouted back, his face turning red with the effort. "The great deceiver who tempted Christ in the desert. Who also tempted Adam and Eve in the Garden of Eden. He's a sly one and he will use intelligence and manipulation to gain power."

He took a moment to sip from a bottle of spring water and launched into his next line with the same vigor as the one before. "I am going to read a passage to you from the Bible and I would like everyone to sit and listen to my words, let them flow over you and let the Holy Spirit touch your heart and soul."

Revelation Chapter 6, verses 7 and 8:

"When the Lamb opened the fourth seal, I heard the voice of the four living creature say, "Come out!""
"Then I saw a pale green horse. Its rider was named Death, and Death's Kingdom followed behind. They were given power

over one fourth of earth, and they could kill its people with swords, famines, diseases, and wild animals."

"The seal was broken on Thursday. The sun burst forth and its poison took eleven percent of our population. Before you start feeling sorry for these abominations, you need to understand that they are the servants of Satan. When they awake, and they will awake, Satan has given them a job to do. They will kill, pass their disease on to others, deceive, and lie to turn you against Jesus Christ. Many will be weak and follow them." Nathan's voice grew louder and he shouted up and down the scale with each phrase. He raised his hands and pointed toward the doors of the church.

"They will demonstrate powers we've never seen before. Unnatural powers that Satan has given them. Now many of you are saying, but *my* husband or *my* wife was a God-fearing Christian." He paused for emphasis, sweeping his intense gaze across the faces of his flock.

"But only God knows the heart of man and Satan took those whose faith was the weakest. You are now going to ask about children, the innocent children. The moment they were touched by Satan they became his servants and they will grow into adult hood and turn against those who loved them. They were touched before birth by Satan's own hand."

The sanctuary was deathly quiet as the evangelist spoke. People were looking at one another in fear.

"I want you to know that there is hope. God has not deserted us. He is with us and guiding our every move. We can defeat Satan. Many will die in this battle and battles to come, but know that you will be a martyred soul and blessed by God. You will rise again to stand before our Lord.

"Revelations Chapter 21, verses 3 and 4:

"I heard a loud voice shout from the throne:
God's home is now with his people. He will live with them
and they will be his own. Yes, God will make his home among
his people. He will wipe all tears from their eyes, and there will
be no ore death, suffering, crying, or pain. These things of the
past are gone forever."

"Forever," chanted the crowd.

"Yes, think of it my brethren and sisters to live under God's eternal light where no darkness can penetrate. To gather with our families and share the riches God is waiting to share with us.

"What does God want from you, you are asking yourselves. He wants you to stand up against evil. We must not allow the people who are under Satan's power to awake. We must kill their physical bodies and set their souls free."

Nathaniel motioned to the choir and they began to sing Hallelujah softly.

"For those of you who have sinned against God, I want you to know it is not too late—His arms are open waiting for you. He will give you the strength that you need to carry out His will."

People began to make their way to the altar and it was so crowded that Nathaniel smiled brightly at them.

"God is pleased and he knows your hearts. For those of you who wish to be literally washed in the blood of the Lamb, our deacons are standing by."

People began to form a line and someone began passing out towels to them.

"I want you to know that God has told me that the police are coming to arrest me today, but they can't hold me behind their bars because the Lord has set me free! They will martyr me by claiming that I am telling people to go out and murder. I'm not telling you that—I'm telling you to kill the spawns of Satan. My death is near and yet it won't be in vain because when Jesus returns, God has promised that I shall be on his right side. Praise God! Praise God!"

Nathaniel reached behind the pulpit and took out a large butcher knife. "You see our former Sister Ellen here who sits in a coma. Her soul now belongs to Satan and we must not permit her to wake up and begin to do his bidding. He grabbed her by the hair and pulled her head up revealing her neck. He held the knife up in the air and began to shout.

"In the name of our Lord God, I send you back to hell."

He then slit her throat. Blood spurted everywhere and he reached out and grabbed her throat by both hands until they were covered in blood.

"In Jesus name I have followed his commandments," he shouted as he raised his bloody hands in the air.

People nearly threw themselves down to kiss his robes and kneel at his feet. Nathaniel touched their heads and later people would claim that a sharp volt of electric went through their bodies.

"Repeat after me, John 3:16:

> *For God so loved the world, that he gave his only begotten Son, that whosoever believes in him should not perish, but have everlasting life.*

"For those of you afraid of becoming a martyr I want you to hear what Revelations 20:4 has to say:

"I saw thrones on which were seated those who had been given authority to judge. And I saw the souls of those who had been beheaded because of their testimony about Jesus and because of the word of God. They had not worshiped the beast or its image and had not received its mark on their foreheads or their hands. They came to life and reigned with Christ a thousand years."

"Amen," shouted the congregation.

"That's right people, together we shall rule on Earth for a thousand years. Once again, the lion shall lay down with the lamb. The earth will see peace it has not seen since the Garden of Eden. A thousand years . . . A thousand years . . . and then we will rise to heaven and join God. The trinity will become one in peace forever. He will reveal all and we will bask in his knowledge. We shall walk the streets of gold and all of mankind will finally be reunited with the one true God."

"I am now going to come and walk among you and pray with you. The choir is now going to sing "Just as I am."" He turned to the choir loft and held one hand palm up toward heaven.

"Just as I am, without one plea,
but that thy blood was shed for me,
and that thou bidst me come to thee,
O Lamb of God, I come, I come.

Just as I am, and waiting not
to rid my soul of one dark blot,
to thee whose blood can cleanse each spot,
O Lamb of God, I come, I come.

Just as I am, though tossed about
with many a conflict, many a doubt,

fightings and fears within, without,
O Lamb of God, I come, I come.

Just as I am, poor, wretched, blind;
sight, riches, healing of the mind,
yea, all I need in thee to find,
O Lamb of God, I come, I come.

Just as I am, thou wilt receive,
wilt welcome, pardon, cleanse, relieve;
because thy promise I believe,
O Lamb of God, I come, I come."

"Did you hear those last words; thou will receive, wilt welcome, pardon, cleanse, and relieve us of the burdens we had had to endure in this life?" Nathaniel's forehead was beaded with sweat as he shouted at fever pitch. "The last verse sums it all up. Let's sing it together."

"Just as I am, thy love unknown
hath broken every barrier down;
now, to be thine, yea thine alone"

Nathaniel Long made it to the front doors as a group of military guards opened the door. He held his hands out in front of him in submission.

The crowd began to get violent, pushing and shoving, and calling for his freedom.

He spoke loudly enough so that his voice could be heard above the crowd. "As I told you earlier, this is God's will and I go with them freely. Continue to sing and pray together and let the Holy Spirit anoint you with his light."

Chapter 16

Boston Mass, Sunday, April 16, 2017, 12:45 p.m.

THE front desk paged Janeen and she went down to greet her guests. Colonel Forester was there and although she had met the guest once before, he reintroduced them. General Corbin Harrison, Dr. Walter Hickman of the CDC, and his director of research Dr. Colleen Giles, Allison Simmons, legal liaison for the sleepers of the occurrence and Dr. Bethany Moore. Although she had met the majority of members when she attended the CDC, it helped to refresh her memory.

"It's a pleasure to have you here," she said, trying to appear as gracious as possible though her exhaustion must show. "Before we take the tour, I wanted to let you know that our neurologists are anxious to meet you. They developed the same theory as you. Dr. Clarke is our Director of Neurology, and his team is anxious to share their results and to work with you."

"We would be interested in collaborating with them. We could use different perspectives on this coma," Dr. Giles said with a smile.

"I know you wanted to take a tour of our tent cities first. I should warn you that it's quiet hectic today. Over a hundred and fifty patient care assistants have begun their training and we have a hundred volunteers working. We have kept the youngest and oldest patients in the hospital because we felt they were at the biggest risk."

"We would like a cross section of at least eight people. Two children, male and female, up to the age of ten, an adult male and female in their twenties, two adults male and female in their thirties, and a male and female older than fifty," Dr. Jenkins said.

"We've started compiling a list of sleepers and I'm sure that will not be a problem," Janeen responded.

"If you'll follow me, I'll give you a tour of the tents."

When they reached the tent, Janeen heard a gasp and turned around.

"I'm sorry, we talk about the number of sleepers, but the magnitude of it all just struck me," Allison Simmons said. "My videographer Jackson will start filming now and edit the video later," she said.

"Each tent has five hundred sleepers," Janeen said. "They each have a feeding tube, IV, catheter bag, and are in hospital gowns and diapers. We reposition them every two hours as well as check their vitals. We'll start passive exercise very soon to make sure no one has contractures as their muscles atrophy. We ran out of EKG machines after the hospital and two tents received them, which is where the volunteers are so helpful. While the nurses are repositioning them, changing catheter bags, and IVs, and they use the volunteers to concentrate on vitals."

"According to Colonel Forester, you had two hundred sleepers in buses last night," the General said in his usual gruff tone.

"Yes, they were taken to the stadium this morning," Janeen said. "We prepped them for care here first however."

"That's quite impressive, Doctor, and something we should share with the public to help boost morale," General Harrison said.

"Our emergency room is overcrowded, but not as bad as yesterday because the other twenty-five hospitals opened theirs today. Mainly it's been bumps, bruises, and stitches. We did have one patient who was in the midst of a heart attack and he's now up in our CICU. He's in the surgery this morning to have four stents inserted. According to our head cardiologist, Dr. Morse, it is a simple procedure for this patient because he's only in his early thirties. But they did have a quadruple bypass yesterday and that patient is in stable condition. The third patient they sent up to CICU had a mild heart attack and is receiving treatment."

"Was he one of the sleepers?" Dr. Jenkins asked.

"No, he was a walk-in yesterday."

They reached the last of the tents and Dr. Hickman turned around to talk to Janeen. "You've done a remarkable job here."

"All of our doctors and nurses did most of the work—it was a joint effort. We had close to seventy-five doctors who aren't even on staff who showed up to volunteer. Everyone has worked side by side and there isn't enough I could say or do to reward them properly.

"Now, if you will follow me, I'll take you to the auditorium."

"If you don't mind, I'd like to get the reactions of the nurses, patient care assistants, health care professionals, and volunteers for my press release this evening," Allison said.

"Let me page Rosemary, the director of nursing," Janeen said. "She can show you around while you interview people. Please get their permission first because quite a few family members that we've found and brought here, are distraught.

"I guarantee the piece will be tactful and that only those who volunteer will be interviewed," Allison said.

General Harrison relaxed into an "at ease" pose and turned to Dr. Hickman. "While the neurologists are meeting, I have some things to review with Colonel Forester. We've made reservations for you across the street at the Hilton and when you're ready, we'll have a guard accompany you," General Harrison said.

"Thank you General. I believe we're going to keep operations here while our scientists continue to work for a solution at the CDC," Dr. Hickman said.

"I need to return to Washington D.C. later this afternoon so I can prepare to give the press conference," Allison interjected. "Is there any chance that—"

"I'm leaving this afternoon, Allison, so you can take the chopper with me," the General said.

"I'll stay the evening and leave tomorrow," Dr. Hickman said. "Although this is a viable theory, we have other teams working on alternative solutions. There's a theory about the electromagnetic storm, but at this point the other scientists we are working with in the US and Switzerland are disputing that."

"I don't know how these mass comas happened, Dr. Hickman, but I've been working on coma theories for the last ten years and I believe I can wake them up. The trials with the rats and monkeys were astounding. We were just getting ready for human trials," Dr. Moore said.

Chapter 17

LAPD had fingerprinted, taken mug shots, and booked Nathaniel Long for murder, inciting a riot, domestic terrorism, and solicitation of murder. Through the entire process, he had maintained a slight smile on his face as if amused by what was happening.

He had refused a lawyer and when they arraigned him the next morning, he pleaded innocent to all charges. The judge denied bail because of Long's ability to leave the country and still Nathaniel smiled.

The judge banged his gavel and down ordered quiet. "I am also ordering a 5150 psychological evaluation."

"I'm not crazy," Nathaniel said, turning his head slightly from the right to the left. "You can't hold me. These are man's laws and I did indeed break them, but they are not God's and He has given me a mission to complete. He is the only one who can set me free. The flock needed to know what God told me. I have followed His commandments and shall sit on His right hand side after the thousand years of peace on earth. We have waited many millennia for the apocalypse and it has finally arrived. How could man have been so blind he missed all the warning signs? The Fourth and Fifth seals have now been broken and it is time for the sixth. Be prepared, there is still time to turn away from your sins."

The judge banged his gavel and called for order and yet he sat mesmerized as Long continued his ranting.

Revelations 6: 12-17:

"I watched as He opened the sixth seal. There was a great Earthquake. The sun turned black like sackcloth made of goat hair, the whole moon turned blood red, and the stars in the sky fell to earth, as late figs drop from a fig tree when shaken by a strong wind. The sky receded like a scroll, rolling up, and every mountain and island was removed from its place. The kings of the princes, the generals, the rich, the mighty, and every slave and every free man hid in caves and among the rocks of the mountains. They called to the mountains and the rocks, "Fall on us and hide us from The Face of Him who sits on the throne and from the wrath of The Lamb! For the great day of their wrath has come, and who can stand?"

Some of his congregates were in the courtroom and shouted, "Praise the Lord, Amen."

"Bailiff," the Judge said loudly. "Remove anyone who continues to disrupt my courtroom."

Nathaniel still displayed his royal stance despite the handcuffs encircling his wrists and secured with small chains to a larger one hanging loose around his waist. His ankles too were shackled and chained to the waist belt. As he shuffled toward the back of the courtroom with a bailiff on one side and a county officer on the other, he pretended to slip and grabbed the officer's gun. The bailiff drew his weapon and was soon joined by another officer who rushed toward them from the row of men in orange jumpsuits, waiting for their turn in front of the bench. The two officers shouted at Nathaniel to drop the weapon and lay face down on the floor, but he only laughed.

"The sun was the key to this passage. Don't you see that those who fell victim must die to stop Satan's work? They pass on the plague to everyone on earth. They will have the power of angels and their wrath will spread throughout the earth in a matter of months.

"Just as God told me, you will make me a martyr and my followers will do the Lord's work. I am ready to meet my creator."

The bailiff fired and Nathaniel fell to the ground. "I go to sit at the right hand side of God," he sputtered as he breathed his last.

His congregants began to wail and the courtroom became a madhouse. Everyone rushed to get out, lawyers and onlookers to perceived safety while the faithful tried to gather around Nathaniel, and sometimes the two collided.

Alarmed by the rush of congregants toward Nathaniel, now lying face down in a pool of his own blood, the officers pulled stun guns and fired them, which created more screaming and chaos.

The bailiff knelt next to Nathaniel and shook his head. "He's gone."

"It is as he said," cried a man in his mid-twenties with an ornate tattooed cross on one beefy forearm. "The time is close at hand. If we allow Satan's people to awaken, then it will truly be the beginning of the end."

Chapter 18

AFTER Janeen had made the introductions, Dr. Clarke grasped Dr. Moore's hand and began to pump it enthusiastically.

"It is such a pleasure to meet you. I've followed your work for the past ten years and your theory on comas is revolutionary. I hope you're not offended, but I brought down eight sleepers and set up an EEG for each of them. The two youngest children's parents are unknown at this time, but I would guess their ages between seven and nine. We selected two males and females, in their twenties and in their thirties according to their driver's license. The final two are in their late fifties."

"Excellent work, Dr. Clarke," said Dr. Moore. "Our tests included rats and monkeys; however, we induced those comas before attempting to wake them up again with the dopamine. We just received approval to begin on human trials. If you don't mind, I'll show you the calculations we arrived at."

Everyone took a seat and Dr. Moore picked up a dry erase marker and began to write on the white board.

"There is something new that we just discovered last night that you should be aware of," Janeen said, as Dr. Moore continued to write.

"The irises of the sleepers are turning gold. We checked them for jaundice and all forms of hepatitis and they came back negative. We also did bloodwork for pancreatic function, and this checked out—and the tests were negative for tumor markers."

"Did the blood work show any anomalies?" Dr. Giles asked.

"Yes, but nothing that would affect the eyes." Janeen handed each neurologist a packet of test results. "We tested their pituitary glands for rate of hormonal activity and we discovered that all subjects are over-producing the adrenocorticotropic hormone (ACTH), which in turn is producing too much cortisol. It is also producing an excessive amount of the growth hormone (GH). At first, I thought it was unusual until we had tested fifty patients and they all had the same overproduction ratios. Their cortisol levels are off the charts. The only conclusion I could come up with is that it has something to do with the over activity in their cerebral cortex."

"Interesting," Dr. Gail said.

"Did you note any facial thickening as well as the hands and feet?"

Janeen nodded her head negatively. "They have no symptoms of too much GH."

"Were these eight of the sleepers you tested?"

Dr. Clarke took over the explanations. "Yes, we tested these eight for every type of blood work possible. We also took an MRI and EEGs. Other than not waking up, they are healthy.

"Now, what I am going to propose may sound ludicrous, but per-haps the over-production of cortisone and GH are why these people went into a coma. I know that NASA believes it was the geomagnetic storm and they could be right, except they aren't addressing why only 11 percent of the world's population became sleepers?"

"Perhaps we can bring someone out of a coma," Dr. Moore said. "If we can test sleepers who wake up, the testing might show us something we're currently missing."

"Excuse my interruption, but I need to check on tent city. If you need me just page me," Janeen said.

Dr. Morris turned away from the whiteboard. "Today we'll work on the calculations of how much dopamine or epinephrine to give them and start the procedure tomorrow. We may start with the dopamine first or we'll test one victim with dopamine in each age group and the others epinephrine. Will someone explain their EEGs?"

"I had Dr. Swartz hook me up and then we did the test subjects," Dr. Clark said. "Their EEG waves were higher than my own which as we know are associated with memory and learning. It also showed they were all in a REM state . . ."

Suddenly the intercom turned on. "Dr. Corbett, code blue in the pediatric unit! Code blue!"

Chapter 19

THE auditorium was on the sixth floor and Janeen ran towards the stairs and made it to the fifth floor. She turned the corner and ran to the window. Rosemary stood inside and in front of her Laureen sat in a chair with a switchblade in her hand, rocking a baby screaming at the top of its lungs.

Janeen took a deep calming breath and entered the ward. "Good morning, Rosemary, Good morning, Laureen. What's going on?"

Laureen wiped tears and snot away from her face with her sleeve and held the switchblade close to the baby's neck.

Rosemary touched Janeen on the shoulder and began to talk in a soft voice. "She won't explain; only that Nathaniel Long, that fundamentalist preacher, said it was the Lord's will."

"Laureen, you know you can trust us. We brought you in off the street and gave you a job and a place to sleep. You've been so wonderful and kind to the sleepers. Will you please explain what you're doing?"

"The baby isn't a stranger, he's my son, and he collapsed just like all those other people. I watched Evangelist Long on the television this morning. I'm one of many disciples that he sent out into the world. He told us to prepare ourselves for the end times because they were near."

"What end times, Laureen? I'm afraid I don't know what you're talking about," Janeen said trying to remain calm. Laureen had the knife too close to the baby's neck to take the knife away from her and she needed to find a way to reason with her.

"It's the apocalypse! The fourth seal was broken by Jesus our Lord and Savior. This morning Evangelist Long went on national television and he said that when the sleepers woke up they would cause disease, war, and famine. He said we had to kill them before they woke up and began Satan's bidding. The military took him away and ended up killing him. God spoke to him directly and told him what must be done."

"Laureen, you are holding the child that you gave birth to. You are his mother and your job is to protect him."

"I am his mother only because the servants of Satan raped me. I loved him although half of him belonged to Satan and now it's my job to make sure he doesn't grow up. He could even be the antichrist."

"Laureen, do you honestly think that God would want you to murder a little baby?" Janeen closed her eyes and tried to remember the verse. "Didn't he say suffer the little children to come to me? I think he was saying that he could save all the children because they were pure and innocent. You are still a child, too, Laureen and it's not too late for him to save you as well.

"Don't you think it's a miracle that Solomon was the first to awaken from a coma? Doesn't that show you how special he is to God?"

Laureen lowered her head and began to pray aloud. "Father forgive me," she whispered.

"What is the baby's name?" Rosemary asked softly.

"His name is Solomon, from the Bible, because he was so wise."

"How old is he Laureen? He looks like you," Janeen said.

Laureen began to sniffle. "He's just turned a year old last week."

Janeen smiled and held out her hand to Laureen. "Look at that, Laureen, you've rocked him back to sleep. May I please take him now so that we can get you some help?"

"If I do this and give you to him, God is going to punish me and send me to hell for not following his will!"

"No honey, God will be happy that you didn't let someone talk you into killing Solomon."

Laureen slowly got up and handed the sleeping baby to Janeen.

"Colonel Forester is here. I'm sure he plans to arrest me now."

Janeen shook her head no. "He'll make sure you get the help you need."

Rosemary put her arm around Laureen's shoulder. "We're taking you to the twelfth floor to speak to some doctors who can help you."

"What about Solomon?"

"We'll take good care of him, Laureen, until you are well enough to take care of him yourself. We are going to do everything in our power to make sure that happens," Janeen assured her.

As Rosemary and Laureen left with Colonel Forester, Janeen looked down at the baby and felt her eyes welling up with tears. He'd escaped the occurrence only to have his throat nearly slashed by his own mother.

Janeen laid him in a crib and removed his clothes and diapers. She removed the feeding tube and catheter, but left the IV still attached. Solomon woke up and looked at her with sleepy eyes. He tried to nurse on her hand and then to suck on his thumb so Janeen pulled the pacifier from his crib.

A beautiful baby, with a headful of thick black curly hair and the longest eyelashes she'd ever seen on a toddler, he also had dark eyes that seemed green in bright light, and a fair complexion. Absolutely perfect. Janeen talked to him while she took his vitals. He cooed, and giggled when she kissed the soles of his feet.

Solomon was the first to awake after a coma and she decided to take him up to auditorium after she gave him a bottle. He drank greedily while she called Dr. Lancaster with the news.

"This is a miracle, I have to call Angela Simmons, and we have to get that child's face in front of the camera. It's a miracle and it will give people hope for their loved ones."

Janeen waited for Rosemary and Colonel Forester to return. They both looked in awe at the baby who was now sitting on her hip.

"Go ahead and touch him, he won't break," Janeen laughed.

"We need three pediatric nurses up here in case the other babies start to wake up. Also a guard so they are protected," Janeen instructed.

Forester smiled. "There are already two on their way."

Rosemary returned shaking her head. "Laureen's in good hands now. This Long wacko has her convinced she's going to hell for not killing Solomon. She kept saying she wanted to die."

"I'm going to take Solomon to the auditorium for the neurologists to examine, and we need lab techs to do a complete blood workup. Rosemary, would you mind staying here until security and nurses arrive?"

"I'd love to and tonight I want my turn rocking the little one! By the way, Dr. Bower the Director of Psychiatry, is evaluating Laureen now and since martial law is in effect, we can keep her as long as necessary. I feel sorry for the lass—she's been brainwashed. That's what they do you know, take innocents who've been abused and convince them they now have a family that loves them. It fuckin' pisses me off."

"From the little I heard on the news, this Long fellow has a lot of followers. A charismatic psycho has the power to reel in many innocent people, people that are in pain emotionally, and convince them of about anything. He uses a few facts and then distorts the truth," Janeen said shaking her head.

"I'm going to go ahead and head to the auditorium. Forester, would you like to join me," Janeen asked.

"I wouldn't want to miss the shock on their faces," he chuckled. "Especially the General. Perhaps we will see another emotion from him rather than gruffness. Be nice to see the man smile."

"We also need a pediatrician to meet us there," Janeen said.

"I've already called them and they are on their way along with Allison and her trusty camera," Forester said with a smile.

Chapter 20

FORESTER opened the door to the auditorium so Janeen could wheel the IV stand through the door. Everyone was still there, including Allison Simmons, who still stood behind her cameraman, taping the remainder of the meeting. When Janeen finally maneuvered through the door, everything became quiet.

"I'd like you to meet Solomon—he's a year old and awoke from his coma. I did a brief external exam and the only thing out of the ordinary is his that his irises are turning gold. The change occurred rapidly because ten minutes before they were green."

Everyone began to shout out questions and Solomon scrunched up his face and began to cry. Janeen held him at her shoulder and rubbed his back in small circles until his tears subsided.

"People," Janeen said softly. "I know this is a monumental moment, but we are dealing with a baby who just woke up from a coma and whose mother just tried to slit his throat. Let's take this evaluation slowly."

A doctor Janeen didn't know sat down on the floor with a fluffy lamb. "My name is Peter Mathews, I'm a pediatrician. Why don't you put him on the floor and let's see if he'll crawl or walk towards me."

Janeen sat Solomon on the floor next to her and he immediately grabbed her leg.

"It's alright, little one, I'm right here with you."

Solomon leaned against her leg while he stood up and reached out his hand. He grabbed her finger and began talking in only a language other babies would understand. She took a step towards Dr. Mathews and he followed her and squealed when he saw the lamb. He let go of her finger and on tottering legs walked to Dr. Mathews.

Dr. Mathews handed him the lamb and he plopped himself down and began to kiss the lambs face.

"I'm going to take blood through his IV and then remove it as it is no longer needed," Dr. Giles said.

The entire room grew quiet as Dr. Giles drew the blood and everyone focused on Solomon.

"Cookie," Solomon said, as his reached out his hand.

"I've got something even better," Dr. Mathews said as he pulled a lollipop from his jacket.

Solomon began bouncing up and down on his bottom.

"Dr. Corbett, if you could lift him to this table, I will quickly examine him while he is occupied with his treat," Dr. Mathews asked softly so as not to frighten Solomon.

Janeen lifted the baby up, talking to him the whole time.

When Dr. Corbett shined a light into his eyes he pushed it away, began to cry, and rubbed his eyes.

"He is overly sensitive to light. Interesting," Dr. Mathews said.

Dr. Mathews listened to the child's heart and lungs and pretended to play a game while he manipulated his limbs. He looked in his mouth and ears and smiled.

"Other than having golden eyes and the sensitivity to light he appears normal," Dr. Mathews said. "He's within the correct weight and height parameters. Perhaps the blood sample will show something—we'll need to wait for the results, of course. I'm stumped—one minute he was still in a coma and then the next, woke up as if he'd just been asleep."

"Did anything unusual happen to him today?" Dr. Giles asked.

"Well, his mother, a volunteer we took under our wings, visited him with a switchblade and intended to slice his throat open, but we know nothing about his upbringing prior to the occurrence."

"How old is the mother?"

"She turns seventeen next week. Apparently, she joined a religious cult whose leader told everyone watching his worship program on national TV to kill sleepers because they would start the apocalypse."

"I saw some of that earlier today. Some of the major networks caught wind of it and included clips in the news. His name was Nathaniel Long and he believed that God sent him a message that the occurrence was the start of the apocalypse and that the sleepers are the spawn of Satan, whatever the delusional term was," Colonel Forester said. "He was arrested on several charges in Burbank, California, but at the arraignment, he stole one of the officer's guns and a bailiff shot him. He didn't make it. Apparently he told the followers that witnessed the incident to carry on."

"We have his congregations all over the US under surveillance. He clearly has a strong psychospiritual hold on these people, and they believed everything he said. Apparently, today's attempt by the teenage mother hasn't been the only religious-based assault. Two people have died at the hands of family members who considered themselves followers, even though they only watched him on television. Long was worth millions. I also ordered additional security at all sites where sleepers are housed and particularly at any tent cities, where security measures are easier to breach," the General said.

Dr. Clarke had observed Solomon the entire time they'd been talking. "You're not going to believe what I just saw him do," he said with excitement.

"Move the toy out of his reach," Dr. Clarke instructed.

Dr. Mathew moved it two feet away and Solomon began talking again. He pointed at the toy and it slid across the floor until it was beside him.

"Oh my God," Janeen squealed.

Dr. Clarke smiled with pleasure. "Let's try something a little more difficult. Janeen take the lamb and stand by the door."

Janeen followed his instructions, turned around, and waved at Solomon.

"Jeeen, Jeeen," Solomon said excitedly.

The next thing she knew, she was standing beside Solomon who raised his arms so that Janeen would pick him up.

Janeen reached down and scooped him up which made him giggle. "Does someone want to please explain what just happened?" She asked in confusion.

"Solomon moved you and his toy across the floor. There are some minor tests we could do but it's too soon to see how powerful he is."

"We need to do an MRI and an EEG while we wait on his bloodwork," Dr. Giles said. "We need to keep this information top secret. If a one-year-old can do this, can you imagine what an adult might be able to achieve. This would cause worldwide panic."

"Regardless, right now he is still a baby and it's time for his nap," Janeen said firmly. "I know he needs testing, but I don't want him made into a lab rat."

"I can't believe I got this all on tape," Allison said.

"We need to speak to the president first and find out what he wants to share with the world. We don't have any answers as to why or how he can move things," General Harrison said firmly.

"We want to give the people hope, not turn this into a spectacle. If anyone from Nathaniel Long's group saw this, it would convince them that they were right and the sleepers all need to die. It would cause mass hysteria and we are just now calming people down. Show him sitting on the floor playing with this lamb and save the other footage for another time."

General Harrison looked tired and yet his mind seemed focused. "Did you get enough interviews and pictures of the tent city?"

"Yes sir, this is going to be one hell of a pick-me-up video," Simmons said with a wide grin on her face.

"I know everyone is swamped with their jobs, but don't you think Social Services should be called to pick up Solomon?"

"No," shouted Janeen, Dr. Giles, and Dr. Hickman all at once.

"We have tons of testing to do on him and he is a miracle, the first victim to awaken from his coma," Dr. Hickman said emphatically.

Janeen tried to talk as Solomon tried to feed her his lollipop. "No one is taking this baby anywhere. It is my intention to have Laureen sign over custody to me."

The moments the words were out of mouth she looked down at Solomon's golden eyes. She had never intended to ask for custody, after all, she was a single woman who worked outrageously long hours and never kept a regular schedule. She did however have the money to hire a full-time nanny, and there was plenty of space in her new house. It had five bedrooms and one of the upstairs rooms would be perfect for a playroom. She would paint it a bright yellow with a print of Noah's ark animals. It would be a perfect play area for him.

"I'll return as soon as I get him down for a nap and perhaps you could wait to update everyone on your progress until I return."

Forester reached out to Solomon and he wrapped his arms around the Colonel's neck. "I guess I'm coming with you," Forester laughed.

By the time they reached the pediatric unit, Solomon was sound asleep. Forester put him gently in his crib and Janeen put a pacifier his mouth. He rolled to his side and pulled the lamb close to his body.

"Janeen, it's none of my business, but why did you just decide you wanted custody? It seems like a rash decision."

"I have no idea why I said that. I just didn't want him raised in a multitude of foster homes; I wanted to give him security and a home he could call his own. I'll go and talk to Laureen in the morning. She has some obvious mental issues and from her lack of self-esteem, I believe she was an abused child. I intend to help her get back on her feet. If I know Rosemary as well as I think I do, she'll take Laureen under her wing."

"What about her trying to kill Solomon?"

"I don't think she would have done it. Whatever brainwashing techniques Nathaniel Long used, wasn't enough to override that she knew right from wrong."

Rosemary entered the pediatric until and smiled. Janeen went to the nurses supply closet and picked up some formula and baby food.

Janeen told Rosemary what happened and she smiled brightly. "I'm so glad you want to be his guardian. I also agree with you about Laureen, no one has ever given her a chance in life and with the right direction, I think we can build her confidence and help her to become independent. I also don't think she should ever see Solomon again, who knows what control this Long wacko has on her and all his other disciples out there."

"Don't worry, Rosemary, we're increasing security around all the victims' locations," Forester said.

"The pediatric nurses are on their way up, four per shift. There was a mix-up earlier and they each believed someone was here taking care of the babies while they took their dinner breaks.

"So far, we have ten newborns that are healthy. I'm afraid they lost another one though. Stillborn and the mother didn't make it either."

Rosemary made the sign of the cross on her chest before continuing. "They're planning another ten C-sections tomorrow. We're going to run out of room so I moved the patients on the fifth floor from the rooms on the left and right and we're converting it to another neonatal unit."

"Well," Janeen said, "I have to get back to the auditorium and find out what the next step is. Page me if you need me."

Chapter 21

WHEN Janeen and Forester arrived back at the auditorium, General Harrison and Simmons had left for the White House. The President was giving a speech at 9:00 p.m., followed by Simmons' video. She had agreed to take questions after the film played.

Janeen felt slightly overwhelmed by the number of people that had arrived. There were fifteen new doctors clustered in groups of twos and threes, and one was using the whiteboard and drawing images of the eyes and their functions.

Dr. Hickman asked everyone for their attention. "Janeen, these are ophthalmologists on staff. Dr. Feldman, the director of the department, is at the whiteboard. He noticed the woman, who died yesterday in surgery in childbirth, eyes had changed colors, and he removed her eyes as their test subject. He is going to explain their theory as to why the victims' eyes are now gold."

"I can't tell you why the eyes are gold, but I can explain their sensitivity to light and what changes have occurred in their visual system. The only other animal species that has this is a butterfly. We refer to this as pentachromatic. Our normal vision allows us to see up to ten million separate hues of colors. With pentachromatic, a butterfly, for instance, can distinguish up to ten billion colors.

"Their eyes have changed. One explanation for this is the retina has five diverse types of cone cells of different shapes and sizes and can absorb different spectrums of the color wheel. The number may be greater than five because the sleepers can also see the wavelength of electromagnet radiation. Their vision has also has a higher range. I am going to use the butterfly as my continued example because they have the highest range we have measured. The Sara Longwing butterfly has a range from 310nm to 650nm where our vision range is only half of that. Once you begin to examine their eyes, their pupils constrict to block out the bright light. Their eyes rarely if ever dilate."

Colonel Forester raised his hand. "So you are telling us that their eyes have gone through a total metamorphosis?"

"Yes they have and we are unsure if the change is complete. They see colors that we never knew existed, at least those we've only conceptualized. They are going to need sunglasses during the day when they go out to block out the sun and the UV rays.

"We will keep studying their eyesight, but it is a total mystery as to how or even why they changed."

"I don't want this information to leave this room," Forester said. "We don't want to frighten the population any more than they already are."

"If someone would please turn out the lights I will use the overhead projector to show you the difference in our eyes and the sleepers'."

The light clicked off and Dr. Feldman put up two slides. "If you will look at their new eyes, you will see the cones have different shapes and sizes. In the human eye, they are all the same shape, but the sizes are large, medium, and small. The reason that I said I am unsure if the transformation is complete is you look at the victim's eyes and you can see what appears to be the beginning of new cones forming."

He enlarged the image and used his laser pointer to point out the new growth. "I count a total of fourteen, if you include the new growth. Until one of them wakes up and lets us examine their eyes this is the most information I can provide."

"Thank you for the presentation, Dr. Feldman," Dr. Hickman said. "I'm going to fly out a few of our Ophthalmologists from the CDC. I would appreciate you sharing your team's findings with them and allowing them to work with you."

"It will be our pleasure," Dr. Feldman said as he gathered his belongings.

Once he left the room there was silence as if everyone was trying to absorb this new information.

Just as Janeen was about to address the dopamine discussion she heard a voice in her head. "Jeeen, Jeeen."

"Well, it appears moving objects is not all they can do. Solomon is calling for me telepathically. Let's watch the President's speech and watch the video before we continue."

Forester followed Janeen to the pediatric unit. Solomon was standing up in his crib and throwing his toys at Rosemary.

"I've tried to pick him up to calm him down, but every time I get close to him, he throws something at me and then brings it back in his crib to throw it again," Rosemary said, flushed from the experience.

"Well, this isn't a good precedence to set. Rosemary, walk beside me to his crib. Solomon reached out his arms to her and she picked him up. He began jabbering away and playing with her hair.

"I'm going to hand him to you now, Rosemary. Solomon, this is Rosemary and she is our friend. She is going to help take care of you when I'm not here."

Janeen leaned over and handed Solomon to Rosemary.

"No," he yelled, his bottom lip trembling. "Jeeen."

He began to suck on this thumb as tears filled his eyes.

"Let's sit in the rockers," Janeen suggested.

They each took a seat and began rocking back and forth. Janeen leaned over and rubbed Solomon's back. "See, Rosemary is our friend," she whispered softly.

His eyes grew heavy and he finally fell asleep.

"I'll put him back in his crib," Janeen said. "We are going to have to teach him to let other people take care of him, but today has been a difficult one for him and he needs his rest."

Janeen put him back in his crib and he opened his eyes. "Jeeen," he said with a smile on his face.

Janeen picked up his lamb and handed it to him; she covered him up, and kissed him on the forehead.

By the time they were ready to leave the pediatric nurses had arrived. She explained a bit about Solomon and swore them to secrecy. "If he wakes up and asks for me, just page me."

"I need to get a few hours' sleep," Rosemary said yawning.

"You've had a long day and you need it. I wanted to ask you something before you go. If you want, I will put your husband in the first set of trials to try and wake up the patients."

"I thought about it, but I think I'd rather wait until the theory isn't just a theory anymore."

"As soon as it's perfected he is at the top of the list."

"Thank you Janeen. Before I get to bed, I'm going to go and check on Laureen. I don't want her to think she's alone. By the way, you look like shit, try to get some rest yourself."

Janeen and Forester stopped at the nurse's station to watch the television. President Mitchell had decided to give his speech after the video. Allison Simmons narrated the video herself:

"Today we went to Boston Mass hospital to visit eleven of the tent cities. I must tell you how impressed I was at the number of volunteers, technicians, patient care assistants, nurses, and doctors working side by side. I expected to see a madhouse like the old television show, MASH; instead, you'll notice that everything is clean and organized. The patients are attended to personally every two hours. Sleepers of the occurrence have clothing, catheters, diapers, IV drips, and many are on EKG machines. Their health and comfort has been the forefront in everyone's minds.

"I have to admit that when I first entered the first tent it took my breath away and I was momentarily shocked and it nearly brought me to tears. We talk in numbers when we are referring to the occurrence or we call them the sleepers. Today I saw a massive amount of people that need our help. I spoke to one of the doctors on staff, Dr. Gregory Lawrence." She turned to a clip that filled most of the screen.

"When there is this many people who are ill, we all pull our weight," Dr. Lawrence said in response to an unrecorded question. "I've changed diapers, did feeding and even emptied catheter bags. So many families have been torn apart by this disaster and some are still trying to locate their loved ones. We want to assure everyone who is watching this broadcast that they are getting the best medical care possible and we have sent pictures and ID's of those who had them to the people compiling the database. We will set up schedules of visitation if you discover your loved ones are here."

The camera panned back to Allison. "This hospital has its emergency room open and have even had to perform two heart surgeries. The maternity ward is full and ten healthy babies were born here today. They will continue performing C-sections tomorrow morning."

Allison turned back to the camera. "I next interviewed a volunteer." Again, an interview scene panned out behind her.

"My husband and daughter are out there somewhere and I can only hope someone is volunteering to help them. I feel as if I am closer to them while I am helping these sleepers. I know that I will find my husband and daughter and until I do, I will spend as much time here helping the best I can. Everyone here works as a team. Being here helping is better than sitting home worrying about something I have no control over.

"The director of this tent city, a Janeen Corbett, has been here for over forty-eight hours and yet she still takes the time to stop and thank us for all we're doing. She worked last night on twenty-five buses that would transport people to the stadium today and she didn't care if she got dirty or what needed to be done, she just jumped in and helped."

A picture of Solomon came on the screen, giggling and hugging his lamb. "This, ladies and gentlemen, is what caring for the sleepers of the occurrence is all about. Solomon, this beautiful one-year-old, came out of his coma this morning and as you can see, he is a healthy, normal child. It's hard to believe he went through anything. I want you to look at his picture and know that the day will come soon when you will reunite with your families. The CDC and scientists all over the world are looking for a cure and we will report to you daily if people start to wake up. Today is a day of celebration, a day of hope, a day filled with promises of tomorrow. This is Allison Simmons reporting to you from the White House."

Allison had decided at the last minute to refrain from taking questions and she gathered her paperwork and left the podium.

Forester and Janeen made themselves comfortable in the nurse's chairs and waited for the President to give his speech.

"I don't know what I was expecting when she was filming," Janeen said. "I thought for sure every negative would be brought to light and instead she gave even me hope."

"I don't have much time to watch television, but everything I've seen before this is all doom and gloom. They even showed one of the sleepers being attacked by rats in Los Angeles and the filmmaker didn't even stop to try to help. Most journalists are bottom feeders from what I've seen the past few days—even that opinion was too generous. Allison did an excellent job and she didn't try to sugarcoat everything or exaggerate it in any way."

Before Janeen could respond, the President walked towards the podium.

"Good evening and it truly is a good evening. We have had our first victim come out of a coma and he appears healthy and alert. More stadiums opened today and now we are in the final stages of our door-to-door searches. Neighborhoods have come together to help the military and it is now a joint effort that is speeding up the process. The American people have shown their loyalty to their country and their fellow man. Certain businesses have reopened under protection of the National Guard and although we have checkpoints along the interstates, trucks are resuming deliveries of much needed food and staples. The Red Cross has opened food banks at all local schools for those who cannot reach grocery stores or who lack the funds to purchase food. If you haven't been able to use an ATM because of bank closures, you can still pick up a food box or sanitary and medical supplies. We ask that every single person donate any surplus personal food or supplies to the American Red Cross or to any military or police checkpoint, so that others who lack these may be assisted.

"Now I come to a topic that has weighed deeply on my mind for many days. I met with thirty major insurance companies today and was told that if this continues for more than a month, they would be bankrupt from paying out medical and unemployment claims. I have decided to use my executive power and offer free medical care to all Americans. Though all Americans have some form of insurance, we don't have a plan set up for socialized medicine beyond Medicare. Congress and the Senate are working night and day to present a bill for my signature. Moving forward, if Americans approve to continue this measure, no American will ever go without medical care again in the United States.

"The rumors coming out of North Korea are true; they are burying peasants who are in comas, alive. The United Nations is holding an emergency meeting within the next few days, but with all countries stretched to the breaking point of running out of the necessary medical supplies, any sanctions would be moot at this point. No one can make deliveries as most countries have banned travel of any form. My heart bleeds for the Korean people. May God have mercy on the souls who are committing this atrocity.

"I again am not going to answer questions tonight as the press secretary is keeping you informed of everything as it happens.

"One more thing I want to mention before I finish this evening. I want to give special thanks to Boston Mass and all the people who are working there. You are a fine example of what being an American means."

Chapter 22

BY the time Forester and Janeen reached the auditorium, a number of people were leaving. Dr. Hickman of the CDC was just coming out the doors.

"Oh, Dr. Corbett, General Forester. We've done our calculations and know which dosage of dopamine we're going to start with. It's been a long day and we want to be well rested before we begin the process tomorrow morning at 6:00 a.m. You two look like you could use the sleep as well."

"Thank you Dr. Hickman, I'll be here tomorrow morning first thing," Janeen said.

"I'm afraid I have to visit the other twenty-five hospitals and will be gone for a few days, Forester said. If you need any help, Corporal Henderson will be here in my stead. I'll have him check in with you tomorrow."

"I'll let you two get some rest, I want to check with the head nurse on duty and find out how the tent cities are doing before I turn in," Janeen said with a weary smile.

When Dr. Hickman walked away, Forester cleared his throat. "As exhausted as I am, I'm not going to be able to sleep. Would you like to have a drink with me in my quarters?"

"I can't think of anything I'd rather do than have a stiff drink. Let me check the tents and then I'll join you."

When she entered the first tent, Janeen saw hundreds of people doing a variety of things with the patients. Helga Schofield saw her and came over.

"If we had this much help in the regular hospital people would run out of things to do," she joked. "Everything is running smoothly. The patient care assistants have had enough training to do what they need to do and the volunteers are repositioning the patients every two hours. We did have an unusual incident earlier—one of the patients actually sat up looked around and then lay back down. I'm keeping a close eye on him."

"Are any of the Neurologists still on duty this evening?" Janeen asked.

Helga shuffled through her paperwork. "Dr. Clarke is still on duty for another hour. I can page him if you'd like."

"Yes, go ahead and page him. I'm going to finish walking the tents and then I'll be back."

The last four tents were empty of volunteers, technicians, patient care assistants, and nurses and Janeen found the silence disconcerting. She stopped occasionally to read a patients chart and was surprised that there was no fluctuation in their vital signs. Even there pulse rates stayed consistent.

When she returned to the first tent, she found Dr. Clarke examining the patient.

"I thought we might want to run an EEG on this patient. It seems that, if only momentarily, he woke up," Janeen explained.

"I agree with you. I'm going to have an orderly help me move him into the surgical suite we've set up for a variety of tests. I'll page you when we get the results," Dr. Clarke said with a deep sigh. "I hope the dopamine works tomorrow. If it does, we're going to have to wake them up in small groups. They're going to be disoriented and feel weak. Explaining all of this is going to be difficult because we haven't the foggiest idea of what's happened. I'm also wondering if they are going to wake up with telepathic and telekinesis abilities like little Solomon. An even a bigger question is what other abilities they might display."

"We have to take it hour by hour, Dr. Clarke."

"Call me Carl—I never did officially introduce myself." He held his hand out, his face animated by an infectious grin.

Janeen laughed. "I think common courtesies went out the window when the occurrence happened. It is a pleasure meeting you, though."

Janeen made her way to Colonel Forester's quarters and the soldier on duty next to the tent door gave her a big smile. "He's expecting you."

When Janeen entered the tent, she wasn't quite sure what she expected, but there was a table covered with blueprints and papers laying everywhere. He had made his bed with military corners, however, and for some reason she found this amusing.

He heard her enter and turned around. "I hope you like bourbon, although I think I still might have a bottle of wine here somewhere."

"Bourbon is fine. My dad drinks bourbon and I learned to like it from him. Don't ever tell my mother, but when I was younger he would always let me have a sip."

"Your father is a doctor if I recall, right?"

"Yes, a well-known plastic surgeon. My mother was one of the sleepers of the occurrence and he's at home taking care of her. He would come and help if I asked him to, but they've had such a close relationship that I won't pull him away from her.

"I tried to convince him to let my mother be one of the first they tried the procedure on to bring them out of the sleep like coma, but he refused. He said that he wanted to wait until the procedure is perfected. I understand his feelings as a physician, but as a daughter, I wish he would change his mind."

"My parents were both killed in a DUI five years ago. I was an only child and I miss them dearly."

"I'm an only child as well. I think our bond is stronger with our parents when we're constantly the center of attention," Janeen theorized.

"What about yourself, do you want children?"

"Well, I've got one now," Janeen laughed. "Yes, I've always wanted a large family, but then again I don't even take the time to date and now that I'm going to adopt Solomon, it's going to be even more difficult."

"Motherhood seems very natural for you."

"I'll be honest; I have no idea of where the words came from when I said I wanted to raise him. It shocked me as much as everyone else in the room."

"Is there a chance Laureen could get better and want custody?"

"Laureen has been abused and we have no idea of what degree. She is vulnerable and Nathaniel Long tried to use that to his own ends. No, she won't want Solomon back. She might want to visit him though, which could be good for Solomon."

The loudspeaker overhead came to life. "Dr. Corbett, please report to surgical room #4."

Janeen wearily rose from her chair. "Thank you for the drink, I'm sorry I can't stay longer. One of the patients sat up earlier and looked around and so Dr. Clarke is running an EEG."

"I understand perfectly. I'll check in with you while I'm gone."

Forester took her left hand in his for a brief moment and gave it a squeeze.

Although it was only a moment of contact, Janeen felt flushed. She chastised herself for taking a simple gesture of kindness as something more. She decided she really needed to start dating again.

When she arrived at the surgical suite, Dr. Clarke was standing outside waiting for her. "I've moved him to the auditorium. The EEG shows that he's in a light coma. I believe he came out of it for a brief moment and that he should be one of our test subjects tomorrow."

"Carl, this is wonderful news," Janeen said. "Perhaps the sleepers will start to awake on their own."

"Under normal circumstances I might agree with you, but it's been discovered that a few of these patients are in deep vegetative states and they'll need a jump start," Dr. Clarke explained.

"I'll see you tomorrow morning at 6:00," Janeen said as she turned to head to the doctor's staff lounge.

She was too wired to sleep and so she took a long shower and slipped into fresh scrubs. Janeen was sitting on her cot drying her hair when there was a knock on the door. Confused as to why anyone would bother knocking—it was a co-ed lounge—she flung her hair back and opened the door. There stood Solomon, naked with a diaper in his hand.

"Dirty," he said and made a face.

Janeen leaned down and picked him up. He wrapped his arms tightly around her neck and gave her a sloppy kiss on her nose. "Jeeen, mommy," he said and smiled.

It was then that she realized what a monumental task she had taken on. Solomon was extremely bright for his age and with his telekinetic and telepathic powers, he was going to need a firm guiding hand.

She wrapped him in her towel and carried him back to the pediatric unit. The minute she walked in the nurses rushed to her side.

"We've been looking for him for a half hour," a volunteer by the name of Kristin said. "We were just getting ready to page you."

"I'll tell you what, I'll dress him for bed, and since he's had such a rough day, I'll pull a cot in here and he can sleep with me.

"How are all the babies doing?"

"Surprisingly well. Earlier they all began to cry at once, Solomon began singing a song that none of us could understand the words to and they all fell back to sleep," Kristin said.

"You are going to have to keep a close eye on Solomon; he came to find me in the doctor's staff lounge. He's smart, but he's still a baby and could get hurt."

"I apologize Dr. Corbett, his crib has a slide panel we can use to keep him inside, we just didn't expect for a one year old to be able to get out of the crib."

Janeen dressed Solomon and one of the nurses had already brought a cot to sit next to Solomon's crib. She picked him up, laid him in the cot, and got in next to him. He snuggled his head into her shoulder and began to suck on his thumb. "Mama," he said tiredly as he fell asleep.

Janeen woke up at 5:00 a.m. to see Solomon sitting next to her patting her on the head.

"Good morning, little one. Now, what are we going to do with you today? I have some important meetings and I can't have you moving me around the hospital like a chess piece."

"I'm not eavesdropping," Kristin said. "But we have some playpens, we could fill one with colorful toys and you could take him with you. I'll prepare a diaper bag for you with bottles and all the other things you'll need. We'll even set it up in the auditorium while you get breakfast."

"Kristin, you are a lifesaver. I need to go get ready, so could you watch him until 6:00 a.m. when our meeting starts?"

"It will be my pleasure," Kristin said holding out her hands to Solomon.

At first, he stuck his thumb in his mouth and buried his head in Janeen's neck.

"Come on little one, I'll only be gone for a little bit and Kristin loves babies, especially you."

Janeen leaned forward and finally Solomon let Kristin take him. "Bye-bye Jeeen Mama."

Her throat closed up and she thought she might cry, but instead she leaned over and kissed him on the forehead.

Janeen returned to the doctor's staff lounge, brushed her teeth, combed her hair, and then realized how hungry she was.

She only had a half hour before the meeting and jogged down the stairs to the kitchen.

Ethel was there with a cart filled with a large assortment of fresh pastries, coffee, tea, and orange juice.

"I was expecting you this morning. I just dished you up a bowl of oatmeal with brown sugar. When you're finished you can take the cart to the auditorium," Ethel said smiling.

"I love you more every day," Janeen said with a big grin.

"Well, someone has to make you eat. With as many hours as you are putting in, you are going to get sick. I'm made it my personal mission to make sure that doesn't happen."

Chapter 23

AS Janeen rolled the cart off the elevator, Dr. Hickman and Dr. Giles were having a rather heated discussion. Janeen cleared her throat so that they would be aware of her presence.

"Ahh, you come bearing gifts," Dr. Giles said pleasantly.

"You ladies go on ahead. I'll roll the cart in."

When Janeen arrived, she noticed that the room was less crowded then the day before. There were the six neurologists and Carl raised a hand in greeting. Dr. Hickman, Dr. Giles, Dr. Moore, and three physicians, Dr. Feldman and two of his ophthalmologists, and Allison Simmons ready with her camera. Although there were now nine hospital beds laid out in a circle with sleepers in them. They had decided to use the auditorium because it was the largest open space in the hospital.

"I thought you were going to be filming the other hospitals today," Janeen commented to Allison Simmons.

"I was, but this is more important. I've sent two of the other members of my crew to cover it. I've never used this camera before, but according to my crew it's full proof."

"By the way, I thought your video was astounding last night. It had me in tears and I was there when everything was going on."

"The President loved it as well; it raised his popularity points by twelve. I don't think that's the real reason he liked it, though—I think it gave him hope that we're going to find a solution to this problem.

"He's under a lot of stress, some undeveloped countries are pleading for our help, and we can barely take care of our homeland. He did insist the medical supply houses worked 24/7 and we're trying to stockpile medical supplies for other countries.

"Also, the United Nations meeting is today. He's hoping we are successful with the dopamine trials to give other countries hope. He has so much faith in this cure that he ordered the pharmacy that makes the drug to put aside any other pharmaceutical orders and concentrate on the dopamine."

Janeen smiled. "I have a lot of respect for our President and I'm glad the government gave him executive power. He saved the insurance companies by covering all health costs with government funds. He makes a speech every night and he's laying most of it on the table and the things he is not would only cause mass panic."

"Well, tonight he has another bit of good news. Tomorrow the victim database will be available for online searches. Also, the database will be displayed on television stations. The other great surprise is that President Mitchell is informing the public that we have five hundred phone volunteers who can look up the information for those who don't use the internet or if it gets bogged down."

"Thank you for the heads up, Allison. I'll set up a rotating visitation schedule. I have a 10:00 a.m. meeting with the other twenty-five Boston hospitals and will make sure they get a schedule developed as well."

Just as Dr. Moore started to begin the meeting, Kristin arrived with the playpen and Solomon. She set him up in one corner of the auditorium and motioned to Janeen that she was leaving the diaper bag.

"Hi Jeeen, mama," said Solomon.

The people in the room began to laugh and Solomon giggled along with them.

Dr. Clarke smiled at Solomon. "After we've have given our test patients their injections, I'd like to give Solomon an EEG and the pediatricians would like to exam him as well."

Dr. Moore did not look amused. "Now if we can began the meeting. After reviewing my research notes, I determined that we had the best results with dopamine, so that is what we will use on these first trials. We have decided to give 10mcg to the younger children. The adults we are giving 15mcg and to the older adults 10mcg. We should see some sort of reaction within an hour, if we see none, then we will increase the dosage every two hours."

The neurologists each took a patient and inserted the medicine in through the IV. A doctor monitored each patient.

Dr. Hickman tried to break the tension in the room. "Did anyone see the news this morning?"

"All I've seen is the president's speeches and I barely had time for that," Janeen responded.

When the rest of the doctors shook their heads no in the negative, Dr. Hickman began to explain.

"This Evangelist Long has really brainwashed his congregation. Apparently, last night in Burbank, some members killed all the older sleepers at a nursing home and then turned the gun on themselves. Security at any facility treating sleepers is going to become even tighter than it is now."

"That is disgraceful," Janeen said. "I thought the general said he had already ordered extra security?"

"The problem is that no one knows how devoted his congregation is or was as the case may be. We know he had many more television followers than just in his church congregation, but what we don't know is if those people are as delusional as his inner circle."

"You know that the true face of mankind is revealed during times of crisis. Some of the nicest people appear to lose common decency, and even kill," Dr. Gills spoke.

"Dirty Jeeen Mama," Solomon said.

Janeen walked over and changed his diaper. He was smart enough that when things calmed down, she could easily potty train him.

"Wait, Dr. Clarke said. The brainwaves are changing patterns in male victim, age thirty-eight, unidentified John Doe, 545. He was the patient last night who came out of the coma momentarily."

Dr. Gills smiled brightly. "Same here, female victim, age eight, unidentified Jane Doe 293."

Patient John Doe, 545 suddenly sat up. He groggily looked around. His speech was a little slurred, like anyone just woken from a sound sleep. "Where the hell am I? Were my wife and daughter hurt in the accident? Someone rear-ended us and that's the last thing I remember."

"Can you tell us your name?" Dr. Hickman asked.

"Yes, it's Jerry Bentworth."

"What else do you remember, Jerry?"

I'm thirty-eight. I have a wife and a daughter, Jocelyne, who is ten. I'm an electronics engineer and I work for Xerox.

"Jerry, this is going to be difficult for me to explain and possibly hard for you to accept, but it started on Thursday," Dr. Clarke said

"When Dr. Clarke finished talking, Jerry appeared to be in shock. Where are my wife and daughter?" he asked with a quivering voice.

"The authorities are working on a database of the occurrence sleepers. We should be able to locate them in the next twenty-four hours. Jerry, I also need to show you something and I need you to remain calm."

Dr. Clarke picked up a mirror and handed it to Jerry.

"What the hell is wrong with my eyes and how come I see things I've never seen before?"

One of the ophthalmologists took a seat by Jerry. "Your eyesight is now extraordinary—you can see electromagnetic light, UV light, and over ten billion colors, whereas a normal human eye can only see ten million. You'll have to use sunglasses outside because your eyes are now super-sensitive to light."

"Do we know why the occurrence happened or why the transformation of my eyes?"

"It has been less than a week, Jerry, and the CDC, along with other great scientific minds, are working on the answers that the world is asking."

"A week? I've got to find my wife and daughter."

"When we are finished here this morning we will take their names and where you were in your accident and see if we can locate them."

Within the next hour, all nine patients woke up and they all asked the same questions.

"I'm sure you all want to find your loved ones and go home, but we need to keep you for observation for at least three more days," Dr. Hickman said.

"Now, we're going to give you something to make you sleep for a few hours because your bodies have been under a great amount of stress. When you wake up, we'll run blood tests, an EEG, and an MRI of your brain. We've been doing that all along, but for the sake of research, we need new test results."

"What happens if we don't wake up again?" Jerry asked.

"We can wake you up again. I can guarantee that," said Dr. Clarke.

When the test patients all fell asleep, Janeen held up her hand to get everyone's attention. "We have millions of people who are going to need an explanation as to what happened to them. I suggest that Allison video an ophthalmologist, a neurologist, and a group of doctors who can explain the side effects of the occurrence. There are too many sleepers to give them the personalized treatment they need. We'll have to schedule any necessary treatments over the coming weeks. I do insist that each victim see a psychiatrist or psychologist before they leave because many may end up suffering PTSD after they are released. Everyone needs to be aware of what to look for. Allison, can you use the director's office and put together a film? I think we should have Forester explain what happened in the occurrence and then a physician, a neurologist, and finally, an ophthalmologist. We can show them the video and have doctors here to answer all their questions, some of them might be afraid of their new abilities and we must reassure them that they are not alone in this. Perhaps, we should also set up group therapy sessions so they can discuss how they are feeling with people who are going through the same thing they are.

"I don't want any more attempts to wake up sleepers until these test patients have been awake for twenty-four hours and until after we've had the opportunity to observe them. We need to see if they have any unusual abilities before they leave the hospital."

"I agree Dr. Corbett—we don't want to move too quickly."

"I have some meetings and I'll be back this afternoon to see how they are doing." Janeen picked up Solomon and his diaper bag and headed toward the pediatric unit.

"Alright little man, Jeeen Mama has to go to work. The next few weeks are going to be busy, but then we are going to work on your bedroom and playroom. We also have to hire a nanny, but don't worry, you get the final selection."

Janeen kissed Solomon on the top of his head and waved goodbye.

The first thing Janeen did was call Dr. Lancaster to explain yesterday's and today's events.

"He literally moved you across the floor?"

"Yes, and to say I was startled would be an understatement."

"We are going to keep the nine sleepers who just woke up to see if they demonstrate any unusual abilities. Solomon could be a fluke. Or we're going to have a lot of explaining to do to the American people. Perhaps I look at things differently, but I believe we've just made a giant stride in human evolution."

"I would agree with you, but you're right, we need to take this nice and slow. I'm about to go in and talk to President Mitchell, so I'll find out what he wants to do," Dr. Lancaster said.

Chapter 24

Boston Mass, Monday, April 17, 2017, 8:30 a.m.

AFTER searching through her office, Janeen finally located the telephone, which she had placed in the top drawer of her desk. Her first call was to her father. She explained everything to him that had happened even though she wasn't supposed to be discussing this with anyone. She could always tell her father anything and it would remain between them.

"I don't think Mom should get the treatment yet until the method has been perfected and we know how the power of telepathy and telekinesis will affect them."

"I agree Janeen. Your mother is right where she belongs and I wouldn't want to try something until it's been scientifically tested. We need to understand why their eyes changed and why they have these powers."

"Dad, you know the little boy I told you about—Solomon. I've decided to adopt him. Now before you tell me all the reasons why it's not a good idea, please listen to my reasoning.

"People are going to treat him differently with his gold eyes and they will torment him even more when they discover his abilities. I have a lot of love to give, Dad and someday I want to have children of my own. I fell instantly in love with him . . ."

"Janeen, quit talking," her father laughed. "I think it is an excellent idea and I know you're going to make a great mother. Wow, I'm a grandpa now. When do we get to meet Solomon?"

"Probably not for a week or so or until Mom is out of her coma. She'd kill me if she wasn't one of the first people to meet him."

After exchanging goodbyes, Janeen decided to confer with all twenty-five Boston hospitals. She initiated a conference call and waited as they signed on one by one.

"Good morning ladies and gentlemen. I'm sorry I haven't been more available to you the last few days, but as you know, we started three additional tent cities, and also prepped twenty truckloads of patients before they were transported the stadium for further care.

"I'm here to listen to your concerns and help you in any way I can."

"Congratulations on having the first coma patient to wake up," said Lee from McLean's Hospital.

"It was an amazing experience and one I hope all of you will experience shortly. I know how busy you are, but I wonder if you could spare an hour and come to Boston Mass this afternoon?"

Suddenly everyone was talking at once about being short-staffed and overcrowded.

Janeen waited for silence. "I know how you feel and I'm meeting with my nursing staff and the doctors to see what we can spare. We have over two hundred and fifty trained patient care assistants and almost two hundred volunteers here so perhaps we could spare a few. I'm not sure if you are aware, but three more tent cities have been added here. We're up to eleven."

"I've only got four," Bob from Boston Medical Center said. "I can make it there around 1:00 p.m."

Lee from McLean's agreed, as well as a woman named Rebecca from Faulkner Hospital and a man named Justin from Massachusetts General Hospital.

"Thank you so much for agreeing to come. For those who can't, I shall make a video to send back to you."

When Janeen hung up the phone, she paged Rosemary and Helga to her office. Helga had probably left for home, but between her and Rosemary, they would figure out the staffing shortage at the other hospitals.

She found herself surprised when ten minutes later both women walked in.

"You just caught me as I was about to leave," Helga said.

"I'm glad I didn't miss you because we need to make some staffing changes and I need your input."

"We have three hundred nurses, two hundred fifty patient care assistants, and approximately two hundred volunteers.

"I know we can't ask these volunteers to go to another hospital because half of them have family here, but what could we spare as far as nurses and patient care assistants?"

"We've started having our lab technicians do some rounds of vital signs, patient care assistants and volunteers on how to take blood pressure, pulse, and temp, so that leaves nurses free for more critical things," Helga said.

"Realistically," Rosemary said. "I think we could spare fifty nurses and fifty patient care assistants. I've noticed now that all the sleepers have routine care, that the nurses seem to have a lot more time to sit and talk."

"Let's send half of each to Massachusetts General and the rest to McLean. They don't have as many patients as we do, but they are smaller facilities and could really use the help.

"Rosemary, if you and Helga can make out a list we can either tell them as a group or personally, it's your call."

"I think we'll call them into the cafeteria, which means we need to hustle before they are off shift," Helga said. "We'll first ask for volunteers and if that doesn't work, we'll just decide for them."

Rosemary picked up her phone and made the announcement over the PA system.

"Do you want me to come with you?" Janeen asked.

"Nah, we will handle this. You handle the doctors," Rosemary said with a wide grin. "They will be much more difficult than the nurses."

"I've decided to ask for volunteers," Janeen said. "I don't want to send too many because we don't yet know what we'll have to deal with when people come out of their comas."

"Dr. Corbett, please report to the auditorium," the loud speaker announced.

"Thanks ladies, I shall talk to you later," Janeen said, as she headed for the auditorium at a brisk pace.

When Janeen arrived at the auditorium, she was surprised to see doctors filling the room.

"They wanted to see what's happening," Dr. Hickman said. "I saw no reason not to let them. This is going to get out sooner or later."

"So the patients all woke up?" Janeen asked. She realized that now that the sleepers were waking up, she could call them patients.

"No, they didn't all wake up. The older two subjects went back into a coma. We doubled their dosage of dopamine and they immediately became conscious again. We're going to monitor them closely to make sure they've received enough," Dr. Giles said.

Janeen climbed on stage and held her hands up. "If I could have your attention, please. I know this day is monumental in science and we have a lot to celebrate, but we still have close to six thousand patients in comas here at Boston Mass.

"I'm glad you're all here because I wanted to call a staff meeting. McLean's and Massachusetts General are short on doctors and I would like to ask volunteers to work at either one." A dozen hands went up in the air and Janeen grinned. "This is wonderful. If you could just write down your names and your cell phone numbers on this clipboard, I'll have the hospitals call you to make scheduling arrangements.

"Now, I don't mean to be a spoilsport, but our patients need rest, so if you could go back to your duties I would appreciate it."

After the gathering of doctors left, there was a knock at the door. Dr. Hickman opened it to see Dr. Clarke holding a naked Solomon with his plush lamb.

"I found him wandering the halls—I think he was looking for you," Dr. Clarke said with a grin.

Clarke put Solomon down and he practically ran towards Janeen. She scooped him up and gave him a big kiss on the cheek. "Guess we'll have to think of something else to keep you in one place," she said with a smile.

Dr. Moore turned to Janeen. "We examined every occurrence patient and they're in perfect health. A few have prior medical issues, of course, but don't seem to be any worse for the wear, so to speak. MRIs came back normal, as did the blood work. We're still waiting on the DNA testing, though. Their EEGs did show an elevation in brain activity that we can't explain."

"Have you tested them for any special abilities yet?" Janeen asked.

"No, we're waiting for you," Dr. Hickman said. "We did ask for current contact information and their immediate family members' contact info so that we can track any patients with special abilities."

"Dr. Clarke, why don't you, Dr. Giles, and Dr. Moore begin the testing?"

"Shut up, why can't you all just shut up?" Her nametag—Miranda—indicated her age—thirty-eight, her marital status, divorced, and that she was the mother of three missing children.

The doctors turned to the test patients at the back of the room, who still sat or lay on hospital beds. Dr. Hickman walked to her bedside and smoothed away her hair from her forehead. "What do you mean when you asked us all to shut up?"

"It's the constant noise. I can hear all of you in my head and I can't stop it. I can even hear what the baby is thinking."

"This is new territory for us, Miranda, so we'll have to learn together."

Janeen watched as Allison filmed further conversation between Miranda and Dr. Hickman.

At least we'll have excellent documentation, she thought.

Dr. Hickman said, "Why don't you look at me and concentrate on what I'm saying and thinking, as if you and I were the only ones in the room."

Miranda looked at him and a smile lit up her face. "It works! I can't hear the other voices."

"Then that's the secret, to focus on one thing at a time. Is anyone else hearing everyone's thoughts?"

All the patients' hands went up.

Dr. Giles made a note on the clipboard she always carried around with her.

"Let's try the same exercise I gave Miranda," Dr. Hickman said. "Concentrate on one person. If you don't want to hear anyone else's thoughts, try imagining you're in a room surrounded by brick walls."

The patients shut their eyes and the room remained quiet for five minutes. Finally, George, a fifty-six-year-old male who had a missing wife, finally spoke. "It's funny—you always want to know what people are really thinking, but believe me, if you could do it, you'd change your mind real quick. I can block out all the sounds around me and I also can read each of your minds individually. What does all this mean?"

Dr. Hickman spoke to the group. "We honestly have no idea why your eyes changed color and why you have these new and amazing abilities. We can fit you with contacts so your eyes are a normal color, but all we can do about your new abilities is to try and help you learn how to use them."

"Let's try something else," Dr. Giles said as she filled seven small paper cups from a large bottle of water. "I'm going to place seven glasses of water on the stage. See if you are able to bring one to you."

Their faces became masks of concentration and slowly, one by one, they each moved a glass into their hand without spilling any water.

"Well, if nothing else, we could work at a carnival," said the patient whose placard read Joe, age 32.

"What else can we do?" Miranda asked.

"We don't know and that's why we need to keep you under observation for a few days, perhaps a week. We don't want to wake up any more patients until we know exactly what they are capable of," Dr. Hickman said.

"That's not all of it, though—you're afraid of how other people are going to react when they find out we have special abilities," Miranda said.

"You're right, Miranda, we are. People are afraid of things they don't understand and your new abilities are potentially intimidating.

We may only have scratched the surface of what you can do."

The little girl, Vivian, spoke so softly she could barely be heard.

Dr. Hickman walked to her bed and sat down on the edge. "What did you say, Vivian?"

"I said I know where my mother is. She's in tent six and her name is Marsha Grossman."

"How do you know that, Vivian?"

"I'm not sure, I just concentrated on her, and I knew where she was."

"You will all have to tell us if you find yourself developing other special abilities because this is as new to us as it is you," Dr. Giles said.

Dr. Hickman stood where he was at the center of the circle of beds. "We don't want to put any undue stress on you, but does anyone remember exactly what happened to them?"

Chapter 25

Boston Mass, Monday, April 17, 2017, 11:00 a.m.

"I remember it perfectly because it was painful as hell," Stephen said. His tag indicated a twenty-two year old male. Single. Parents missing.

"Describe what happened to you, Stephen," Dr. Hickman said.

"Everybody calls me Steve," he said, smiling suddenly as an afterthought. "It was like getting hit by a bolt of dry ice. Cold and yet it burned at the same time. There was a bright flash in front of my eyes and that's the last thing I remember."

"What about you Vivian, what did you experience?"

"Similar to what Steve described, but it felt like someone was drilling through my head and pouring ice water inside. That's when the pain came, I felt like I was boiling from the inside out," Vivian said with a small tear running down the right side of her face.

Dr. Giles began to hand out a tablet and pen to each patient. "It's important when we've had a traumatic experience to write it down in our own words. It helps us to face our fears and to know that we overcame something that could have killed us. I want you to keep a journal and write down everything that comes to mind about your experience. If all you can think of is your favorite flavor of ice cream, then start with that."

"Um, icream, want," Solomon said from Janeen's arms.

Joe sat up and crossed his legs. He began to slowly levitate above his bed. "Hey, look what I can do. Now if I just had a car like this, I could miss the morning traffic rush!"

Steve didn't look too amused. "Seriously, Dr. Hickman, how are you going to explain us to the world?"

"I'm working on a plan, Steve, but of course we've never had anything quite like this happen to large numbers of people. Even your friends and family are going to find it difficult to deal with . . . We can't even tell you why it happened to you. It will take a decade to study the millions of sleepers' DNA samples to check for changes, and then again, it might have absolutely nothing to do with DNA. As physicians and scientists, we want to give you answers, but we're starting with very little information."

"So you can't even tell us if this is going to happen again?" Grace, age thirty-six, spoke with a catch in her voice.

"I wish I could answer that question as well, but I can't."

"What about aliens, has anyone considered that?" Hal, a small boy spoke up for the first time, His tag indicated that his parents were missing.

Dr. Hickman took off his glasses and rubbed his eyes. "Every theory in the universe is under consideration, but according to NASA, there were no unknown anomalies in space except the solar activity about forty-eight hours prior to the time of the occurrence."

"I'm only eight. What does anomaly mean?"

"It means something out of the norm, something strange or difficult to classify."

Janeen walked over and stood in the circle of beds. "You've been through a lot in the past five days, but I don't think you understand the magnitude of what has happened on Earth. If you will all put on your robes, I'll give you each a pair of sunglasses. Your eyes can no longer tolerate bright sunlight. Before you leave us, we'll have special contacts made for you to block out the sun's ultraviolet rays and to cover your gold irises, if you want them covered that is."

While everyone was getting ready, Janeen called the pediatric unit and asked Kristin to bring a diaper and some clothes for Solomon. "Yes, it's alright. We'll find a way to keep him in one place later. I'm in the auditorium."

"Does everyone feel strong enough to walk or would you prefer a wheelchair?" Janeen asked.

Dr. Giles normally cheerful expression turned sober. "Do you really think this is a good idea Dr. Corbett? They've only been out of the coma less than a day."

"Yes, they need to understand the magnitude of what has happened. They feel isolated and they need to know they are not alone."

"Then I insist we use wheelchairs."

"Alright, give me a moment."

There was a knock on the auditorium door and Kristin walked in carrying a diaper bag.

"Excuse the interruption; I've brought him clothes and a bottle. He missed his ten o'clock feeding."

"So the baby is a victim too?" George asked.

"He was the first awake and he woke up on his own," Janeen responded as she picked up the phone to call the emergency room nurses' station.

"Yes, we need nine wheel chairs and nine orderlies or aides at the auditorium. We'll need them for approximately an hour."

Kristin handed Solomon his bottle and was putting a diaper on him when he abruptly yelled "NO."

The diaper flew out of Kristin's hands and landed across the room. Janeen walked over quickly to see what the matter was.

Kristin's face had drained of all color and she stepped back a foot. "He doesn't want the diaper," she stuttered.

"Perhaps he's already potty trained," Janeen mused. "Let's just dress him in his clothes and see what happens."

"Are you sure?" Kristin asked with a quivering voice.

"For goodness sake," Janeen said. "He's just a baby."

Kristin began to dress him and he began talking to her. No one could understand what he was saying, but he seemed quite animated.

When Kristin finished, she set him on the floor and he stood up, walked to Steve, and held up his arms.

Without saying a word, Steve picked him up and Solomon began talking once again.

"He's saying or thinking rather, that I am familiar to him and he wants to know if I want to play. He likes my face and he is telling me not to worry. Well, that's as close of an explanation I can make considering he's a baby."

Steve put Solomon on the floor and he walked to Janeen and took hold of her hand.

"He's now telling me that you are Jeeen, his new mommy. He's also potty trained and that's why he keeps taking off the diaper," Steve said.

"What a smart boy you are. Solomon and yes I am your new mommy," Janeen said as she picked him up.

They waited for fifteen minutes and finally the orderlies arrived with the wheel chairs. Janeen instructed them that the group would visit the tent cities.

When they arrived at the first tent, the group got quiet.

"Just imagine that the Staples Center, the Orange Bowl, the Rose Bowl, and every other large stadium are filled with sleepers. Every hospital in the United States has tent cities like the ones you see here. Other than Solomon, no one woke up on their own and stayed awake. George became conscious for a brief moment, but fell immediately back into his coma," Janeen explained.

"They are all dreaming the same thing," Hal said with a shudder.

Dr. Hickman's eyebrows shot up. "Explain what you mean, Hal."

Miranda reached out and touched one of the victim's feet. "They are all looking at the same thing. They are standing in a desert filled with red sand. The wind is blowing and they are finding it hard to believe. The sky is a mixture of black and red swirls. The sun is almost blocked out, and two moons that seem close enough to touch are above their heads. They are almost crying and they feel a sense of desolation. There are trees in the distance, but they are barren of leaves. This is the place of death."

Miranda moved her hand of off the man's leg and wrapped her arms around herself to try to ward off the chill.

Simmons focused her camera on Miranda. "Do you know where they are?" she asked.

George tried to stand up and the orderly gently pushed him back in his chair. "It is either where they have been or where they are going. They can't survive in either place. They must change so they can adapt to their environment. The metamorphosis is painful and their lungs are reforming themselves so that it filters out the sand. Their eyes are growing a third lens to protect themselves from the wind. They are kneeling now, in the sand, holding both hands against their head as it transforms, so that their brain can expand . . ."

Dr. Corbett reached over and touched George's shoulder. "No

more today, George. You have tired yourself out enough for one day."

"They are in hell," Miranda said.

Steve stood, shoving aside the orderly. "We can wake them up from their deep sleep. Let us free them from the hell they are in."

Dr. Hickman put his arm around Steve's shoulder. "We don't want to wake them just yet, Steve. They have no place to go and we still don't understand all the abilities you possess. If they were to all wake up at once, it might cause mass chaos."

"You are only speaking part of the truth. You are afraid of us and what we can do."

"I am not frightened, only curious," Dr. Hickman answered.

The intercom paged Dr. Corbett and she was glad for the reprieve. What George said had scared her and she could hear the truth in his words.

"We have four directors from other hospitals today who would like to meet you. Orderlies and aides, please return our patients to the auditorium."

"You mean like a freak show," George said bitterly.

"Not at all. These scientists wanted to meet the first group that came out of the coma. If it offends you, I will cancel the meeting."

"I say no," Steve said, holding his hand in the air.

All the remaining hands went in the air.

"I will reschedule when you are more comfortable. If you will excuse me, I do need to give them a tour of tent city."

Chapter 26

"HELLO, I'm Lee from McLean and this is Bob from Boston Medical. I'm sorry, but the other two doctors had emergencies to attend to at the last minute."

"I'm sorry, doctors. I'd planned to introduce you to the first patients who became conscious, but they've had a stressful morning and declined to see you. However, I do have Solomon here, who was the first and only patient to spontaneously awaken."

"Solomon, why don't you say hi," Janeen encouraged.

Surprisingly, Solomon stretched out his arms for Lee to hold him.

"Wow, I am impressed," Janeen said. "He likes you. He hasn't gone to anyone willingly except me and another one of the coma patients."

"I do have some good news for you. I have a list here of fourteen doctors who are willing to transfer to your facilities and a list of fifty patient care assistants, twenty technicians of varying specialties and sixty nurses."

"I can't tell you how much this will help," Bob said. "Do you mind if we take a tour of your tent cities?"

"Of course. Come this way. Oh wait, I'd like to introduce our Director of Nursing, Rosemary Stiles. She keeps this place running like a well-oiled machine."

Rosemary turned from her work and smiled. "It's a pleasure to meet you, doctors. Would you like me to take Solomon and put him down for his nap?"

"That would be great. Thank you, Rosemary."

Dr. Lee handed over Solomon who made a smacking kiss noise.

"He's adorable, what is going to happen to him?" Bob asked.

"I'm going to adopt him," Janeen said with pride.

"My, you've been a busy woman."

"His mother is mentally ill and has no family. Solomon has special abilities now and I think adoption is a perfect fit for all of us."

Janeen explained the special abilities that the coma patients had awakened with and how their eyes had changed.

"This is going to complicate matters," Lee said.

"People are afraid of things they don't understand and with millions of people with these special abilities, powers actually, some people without these will be terrified."

"Yes, we know. That is why we are trying to determine everything we can about what they can do. The President has a special panel that is going to determine how to handle this. My supervisor, Dr. Lancaster, is on it."

"Oh yes, I met him last week," Lee said. "Seemed professional and on the ball, take no prisoner type of man."

"Well, luckily I haven't upset him yet," Janeen said laughing. "Let me give you a tour of our eleven tent cities."

Both doctors seemed impressed with the organization and level of efficiency of the tent city at Boston Mass. Bob asked Janeen if she could come to Boston Medical and offer him some suggestions. They made an appointment for Wednesday afternoon.

As Janeen was escorting them to the front door, her eyes opened in surprise. There were thirty people picketing the front of the hospital with signs that read, "The apocalypse is upon us," "The antichrist must die," and "Destroy the coma patients."

"I hate to cut our visit short, but I need to take care of this," Janeen said as she shook both of their hands. The soldiers at the doors will escort you to your cars.

The military was now lining the sidewalk in front of the hospital, but the picketers had scared away any patients headed to the emergency room. Corporal Henderson entered the hospital and asked if everything was all right. He said that trucks were on the way to remove the picketers, per martial law. "The country is in a state of emergency; gatherings and picketing are against the law in time of crisis—"

Before he'd finished his sentence, a barrage a rocks came through the front windows shattering glass everywhere. Janeen and Corporal Henderson were standing close to the doors and a rock hit Janeen on the forehead. Just as she turned, with blood blurring her vision, she saw Solomon running towards her screaming at the top of his lungs, "NO, NO, Jeeen, Mama, Jeeen."

She threw her body forward to protect him from any rocks when a brick hit her on the back of the head. Her last thought was to keep Solomon safe.

Chapter 27

Boston Mass, Tuesday, April 17, 2017, 3:00 a.m.

THE bright light shining in her eyes was causing her to have a pounding headache. Janeen pushed the object away from her face and tried to sit up.

"Janeen, it's Dr. Giles. You have a minor concussion and you had to have six stitches on your forehead. You were hit by a rock and then a brick. I'm going to help you sit up, but please take it slow."

Although her head pounded and the lights in the room seemed too bright, Janeen allowed Dr. Giles to help her pull herself into a sitting position.

"Solomon," she croaked.

"He's right here in the bed beside you," Rosemary said. "I couldn't calm him down so I made him comfortable with his lamb and he just fell asleep. Corporal Henderson had to have a few stitches himself, but he's back at his post."

"What about the picketers?"

"They were all arrested and charged with a dozen different things. The guard is surrounding the hospital now. How's your head?" Rosemary asked.

"Just like someone slugged me in the head with a brick. Who put in the stitches?"

"Dr. Clarke was on duty in the ER and insisted on doing it himself. Personally, I think he has a crush on you."

"Please don't make me laugh, my head hurts too much. But when things calm down there are a few attractive doctors I'd like the dirt on," Janeen laughed.

"You have a choice—I can give you codeine or Tylenol—we don't want to give you anything stronger with the concussion," Rosemary explained.

"I'll take the Tylenol."

"Give me a few minutes while I go get it. You have your first visitor—Forester came back when he found out what happened and he's been waiting an hour for you to wake up."

Janeen heard a deep cough and looked up to see Forester, hat in hand.

"I came back when I heard; I should have circled all the hospitals from the beginning. It wasn't a good judgment call on my part."

"You can't blame yourself for those wackos. I do think the sleepers need more protection though."

"It's already been handled. How do you feel or is that a stupid question?"

"I have a splitting headache, but other than that I'm fine. I probably needed the nap anyway. I keep skipping my power naps."

"Well, you missed an interesting presidential speech this evening. President Mitchell announced that those who had woken up from the comas are exhibiting unusual side effects."

"Side effects?" Janeen said with a laugh and then held up her hand to her head.

"He mentioned telepathy. He skipped them levitating object and

184

themselves. I also heard that they know what the other coma patients are dreaming about and that they say they can wake them up."

"Wow, pass out for a few hours and news travels fast. So what is the President planning to do, especially now that we have two ways to wake the occurrence patients from their comas?" Janeen asked.

"President Mitchell, General Harrison, Dr. Lancaster, Dr. Walter Hickman of the CDC, Dr. Giles, Vice President Pro Tempore Jared Smith, and Lillian Daniels from NASA are all due here day and they would like you to sit in on the meeting."

"They don't want to wake them up, do they?"

"It's under discussion. They want a thorough analysis of exactly what they can do before they wake up thirty-five million people. It's not their abilities as much as how to get unaffected people to accept the change without going into a panic.

"Nathaniel Long's group, who showed up here today, is saying they all should die and they're willing to die themselves to make sure it does. To make matters worse, there are other evangelical Christians who are jumping on the bandwagon and saying this is the start of the apocalypse."

Janeen shook her head. "People are gullible when they're afraid. They cling to any explanation that allows them to feel in control or that they think explains the unexplainable. Some people want someone to blame during a time of crisis instead of pulling together."

"I do have good news, though," Forester said. "The space launch went well today and will return tomorrow with the astronaut in a coma."

"That *is* good news. Has Lillian Daniels said anymore about the geomagnetic storm?"

"I'm out of the loop on that one. I brought you back a wonderful bourbon, but I didn't think it was quite appropriate to bring it to you here."

Janeen began to laugh. "It would have been the perfect gift."

"Jeeen, Mama?"

"It looks like you have someone else who couldn't wait to see you," Forester said with a smile.

He picked up Solomon and sat him next to Janeen.

Solomon's eyes filled up with tears and he got up on his knees, leaned over, and kissed the stitches of Janeen's wound. "Boo- boo," he said.

Janeen wiped the tears from his eyes and smiled. "Mama's fine," she said and pulled him close to her and patted him on the back.

He sat up and smiled. "Boo-boo," he said.

Janeen touched her forehead but couldn't feel the stitches.

Forester's eye grew wide and he reached for the mirror on the rolling table. He handed it to Janeen without saying a word. She looked in the mirror, at where the stitches should have been, and all she could see was a small pink line.

Solomon smiled, laid down next to her, and immediately fell asleep.

Janeen pointed toward a cabinet on the wall opposite her. "Could you hand me a Band-Aid from the cupboard over there—it should be on the top shelf. You must promise me you won't tell anyone about this. If the government finds out that the coma victims can heal on top of their other abilities, I'm not sure how they would react."

"It's my obligation to tell the General, but I won't say a word otherwise. We'll keep this between us. You see, I'm afraid that these people might be experimented on to discover how their abilities could help the United States in times of war. It's my perspective that we should wake them all up and then deal with the consequences. Either way, there may be confusion and fear. At least if conscious, these people would have a say in what decisions are made about their lives. There are too many of them to be considered a small minority."

"They already don't trust Dr. Hickman and probably me after I wanted to introduce them to other hospital directors."

"We won't say anything about this, but it is phenomenal— telepathy, levitation, the ability to heal—and who knows what else they are capable of!"

"According to what they said today, the people who are in a coma are suffering horribly," Janeen mused. "They're in the middle of a physical metamorphosis so that their bodies can adjust to a new world."

Forester rubbed his stubble covered chin. "I've always been a man who saw the world as black and white, but these past five days have changed me. I now know that just because I can't see something doesn't mean it doesn't exist. That's a big change for a forty-year-old man."

"I'm a scientist who has lived by facts and even I am finding all of this difficult to accept," Janeen said. "We've just made a giant evolutionary step into a new paradigm."

Chapter 28

Boston Mass, Tuesday, April 17, 2017, 6:00 a.m.

JANEEN felt a small hand patting her face. "Jeeen, Mama, peepee."

With a smile on her face, Janeen opened her eyes to a smiling face. She sat up and swung her feet over the side of the bed. She picked up Solomon and took him to the restroom. When she tried to pick him up, he squirmed away.

"Big boy," he said as he lifted the toilet lid.

Once he was finished, Janeen held him up to wash his hands. When she handed him a paper towel, he dried his hands and threw away the towel in the garbage can. He held up his hands. "All done," he said with a big grin.

"You *are* such a big boy. What's say we go and let mama get dressed and then get something to eat. I think you are going to like oatmeal."

Janeen held Solomon's hand and they slowly walked to the doctor's staff lounge. Dr. Clarke had just finished putting on his scrubs when she walked in.

"How's the patient this morning?"

"Carl, you did a fabulous job—I'm not even going to have a scar. Would you mind watching Solomon so I can get a five minute shower?"

"Tell you what, I'm on the way to the cafeteria, how about you shower and meet us there?"

"That is so generous of you. I won't be long."

Janeen jumped in the shower and quickly washed her hair and hopped out. She trusted Carl with Solomon, but with the baby's abilities, she wasn't sure what he might do next. When she reached the cafeteria, Carl had set Solomon in a booster seat and given him a banana.

"I wasn't sure what he likes to eat, but he definitely likes the banana," Janeen said as she took a napkin and wiped Solomon's face.

Janeen grabbed a cup of coffee and two bowls of oatmeal. When she returned to the table, she set the bowl and a spoon in front of Solomon. He carefully picked it up and only managed to get half of the oatmeal into his mouth.

Carl began to laugh and Solomon joined him. Janeen took the spoon and began to feed him and he didn't complain. He kept saying "mmm, mmm".

When he finished, Janeen quickly ate her own.

"Thank you for all your help last night and this morning. I need to see the sleepers in the stadium. Correct that, they are now patients," she said with a smile.

"Do you want me to take a look at your stitches?"

"Nope, I checked them this morning and it looked like they had already started to dissolve. I'm a fast healer."

Janeen felt guilty for lying, but she had to protect Solomon's secret at any cost.

She arrived at the auditorium at 7:15 a.m. just as the patients were finishing their breakfast.

"Morning doctor," Steve said.

"Good morning, Steve, everyone. I wanted to get here early so

I could talk to you before anyone else arrives."

"You're here to tell us the president is coming and his committee of people who are going to decide what to do with us," George interjected before she had a chance to speak.

"Well, I can see your telepathy is getting stronger. Are there any other secrets I should know about, just between us of course?"

"Solomon healed the concussion and the stitches on your forehead," Miranda said.

"You know, it's going to be difficult to have a conversation with you if you don't let me get a word in edgewise," Janeen said with a laugh.

"I'm excited," Vivian said. "I'll be the only kid in my class that got to meet President Mitchell in person. Do you think he'll let me take a picture with him?"

"I think he will, Vivian, and I'd like a copy of it."

Sam, a man in his fifties, spoke for the first a time. "If this plays out like it does in the movies, they're going to want to study us and keep us under wraps. Now Janeen here isn't like them, she has Solomon, but even if she didn't, she cares about people. The way I see it, the world has just had the biggest change since the dinosaurs. We need to have a plan, because I don't want to wake up one morning in some compound after I've been drugged and I also don't want those weirdo religious nuts coming after me. It's not like we have a lot of choices here."

"I say we wake everyone up, there is strength is numbers," George said.

Janeen shook her head. "George, I'm not so sure. That might seem like a threat too many people and many would become defensive. That's not a good negotiating position."

"Can we please wake up my mommy, please," Vivian said, tears running down her face.

"I don't give what a fuck they say today," George said. "We are waking up Vivian's mom."

Janeen sighed. "Alright, here is my first suggestion. Let's get these beds out of here and you each sit in an auditorium seat. I'll remove the IVs and catheters—you don't need them anymore."

Janeen used the phone and called nursing. "Have our test patients had their belongings labeled? Oh, I didn't look there, thank you. If you can, please send someone up to the auditorium to move these beds."

"Apparently, your belongings are on the back row of seats. Get dressed as soon as possible. In the room next door is a shower—in fact, this floor has showers in each room. Go take a shower, wash your hair, and let's meet the president as if we were here to listen to an election speech. We will demonstrate a show of support."

While Janeen was busy, she'd put Solomon in his playpen. He was now rotating the colored blocks above his head and pointed to each one. The only ones he missed were red and green—he kept mixing those two up. Janeen picked up a red and a green block. "Red," she said, handing him the block.

"Red," he repeated back.

"So what is this color?" she asked, handing him the other block.

"Green," he said, bouncing up and down.

"You are so smart!" Janeen leaned down to kiss him. He wrapped both his arms around her neck and gave her a sloppy kiss on the cheek.

By eight o'clock, the first patients to survive the occurrence were all sitting in the auditorium looking as if they were going to work and school, dressed in the clothing they'd worn on that fateful Thursday.

"We have an hour before they show up," Janeen said. "How do you wish to handle the meeting?"

"We've elected Sam as our spokesman," George said. "He's an attorney and we aren't going to make any plans until we know what they are proposing. It's all guesswork at this point."

"I do have one suggestion for you," Sam said. "I wouldn't let Solomon be here for the meeting. He can't control what he does."

"I would tend to agree with you, but President Mitchell made it a point that he wants to meet Solomon and he's too young for me to explain to him to not do what comes naturally to him."

Chapter 29

Boston Mass, Tuesday, April 17, 2017, 9:00 a.m.

THE intercom paged Dr. Corbett at 9:05 a.m. and she gave the group a thumbs up and went to the main lobby. President Mitchell, General Harrison, Forester, Dr. Lancaster, Dr. Walter Hickman, Dr. Giles, Allison Simmons, Vice President Jared Smith, and Lillian Daniels from NASA were all there, and the lobby had twenty Secret Service agents in dark suits, gazing around and periodically talking into earpieces.

"Good morning Mr. President," Janeen said cordially.

"Dr. Corbett, it is a pleasure to meet you. I hear your tent cities are the best in the country. You're an exemplary example to all the directors, which is something I wish to discuss with you after the meeting," he said.

The president studied her a moment before continuing. "I believe we all know each other. Perhaps we can visit with our newly awakened coma patients. I've been looking forward to it."

Janeen led them to the auditorium and when she opened the door, she could see the shock on Dr. Hickman and Dr. Giles' faces.

All the patients stood up and Sam moved forward a step. "Good day, Mr. President. I'm Sam Myers, Attorney at Law at Myers, Ramsey, and Kearn."

The President shook his hand and as he introduced the patients, the President shook their hands as well.

"To my right, Mr. President, is Vivian—she is eight years old and her mother is in tent number one in a coma. Vivian was anxious to meet you today. She would appreciate it if you take a picture with her so that she can show her classmates. Next, we have Hal Christian, age ten—his parents are missing. Miranda Monroe, age twenty-seven, a book editor. Stephen Collins, age twenty-two, a student studying quantum physics. Joe Smith, age thirty-two, a truck driver. Grace Anthony, age thirty-six, a stay-at-home mom. Jerry Henry, thirty-eight, a banker. George, fifty-six an accountant, and lastly, Veronica Baker, forty-one, a sales manager at Macy's. As you can see, we are quite a diverse group of people."

"It's a pleasure to meet all of you," President Mitchell said. He looked at each face as he spoke with an amiable smile.

"I'm not sure exactly what I expected—you all look so healthy. I believe, however, that one of you is missing."

"That would be Solomon and he's taking his morning nap," Janeen explained.

The President introduced everyone in his group and suggested that everyone have a seat. Janeen had arranged for a table and chairs and placed them in the semi-circular stage at the front of the auditorium, facing the patients.

The President took a deep breath before speaking. "I wish to say on behalf of the American people how happy we are that you awoke from your coma undamaged. You did however awake with some rather unusual abilities and that is a cause for concern. It's only been a few days and I'm not sure you are even aware of what you are capable of."

"Mr. President," Sam said. "We have you at a disadvantage, I'm afraid. We can read your thoughts so if this is going to work, you need to forget all the nice civilized words and just lay your cards on the table."

The President raised his eyebrows and nodded in agreement. "We would like to take you to an undisclosed location and run tests on you to see what all you can do. This is going to terrify the public and we have to find a way to tell them that is not going to start a panic."

Sam turned and smiled at the other patients. "Not to be offensive, sir, but I believe when you discover all we are capable of we would never been seen again. We'd become lab rats and our disappearance would be something along the lines that we all died. There are over three million people in comas, in the United States, Mr. President. You can't eliminate them all.

"I do apologize for being brusque, but our lives are on the line here. We can wake up all the coma patients without the use of dopamine. We can't be worried about what our friends and neighbors think. They will have to adjust, as will we. We are just as scared as you are. We haven't even had the chance to reflect on what has happened to us or why. Our biggest question, is it going to happen again? How? Why us? What made us susceptible?

"Our lives will never be the same—I cannot be a defense attorney knowing what the jury is thinking, that is unethical. We are all going to have to make major adjustments in our lives."

President Mitchell's face assumed a grave expression. "I wish I could say everything that you just said is incorrect, but I would be lying and you would know it. You are right, we can't eliminate over three million people, nor would we want to. We hoped to keep them asleep long enough to figure out how we can help the rest of the world adjust to these changes. But if I am honest with myself, I would have to say that many won't adjust—they will always be suspicious of you.

You do realize that quite a few religious zealot groups want to see you dead?"

"Yes, we are aware and we know when we leave here that we may be a target for a long time. Mr. President, you woke up your daughter yesterday—don't you think there are a million parents out there who want their children back as well?"

"How did you know . . . of course you knew."

General Harrison stood up and began pacing the room. "One of the military's greatest fears is that countries who are not our allies will find a way to use these powers against us."

"That may indeed happen," Sam said. "But we are patriots and most of those in comas are patriots; we would never stand for someone using these abilities against our country. You are also forgetting that they have coma patients as well. There's nothing you can do to control their abilities.

"We have a proposal for you. We will let you take us for one week to run all the tests you want, but before we go, we insist on waking up the six thousand people here. We want to spend some time with them to help them adjust and then you can take us wherever you want.

"While we are gone, they will begin waking up the rest of us. You can make a speech about our abilities; we will even allow you to video-tape us. We can show others we are not a threat to their way of life. Half of them will live in fear of us or envy us; the other half will adjust to the new changes. We will have children that will all in likelihood inherit our abilities and in four generations everyone will be able to do what we do."

"We don't need your permission to take you," General Harrison said. "We are under martial law and the President has executive power to do what he thinks is best."

"General Harrison, I know that you are an excellent General and you too are a true patriot, but don't you think we knew this already?"

"At 11:00 a.m. four different news stations are coming to interview us and I've told them if we don't appear that we have been taken against our will."

"You smug son of a bitch," the general growled.

"Sit down, General, please." The president said wearily. "They outplayed us and no one would believe that something mysteriously happened to all nine of them. We are not murderers or kidnappers."

"Ms. Daniels," Steve said. "I cannot explain how I know what I'm about to tell you, but I do know that the electromagnetic storm and the solar flares had something to do with our transformation. It is not the first time in history, either, and won't be the last. We were given the ability to eventually morph into a being that could survive on a planet much different than the one we live on now."

"What else do you know," Lillian asked.

"During our week of testing, I would be more than happy to sit down with you and explain what knowledge I have. Perhaps if we know what is going to happen, we can stop it."

"Mr. President," Sam said. "Do you want to address the press first or would you prefer to have time to make a more formal announcement? As I said before, we are willing to show the American people what we can do in a non-threatening way. Actually, Solomon has more abilities than we do and when we wake up the six thousand we have no idea of what they are capable of doing."

"What can Solomon do?" asked Dr. Giles.

Sam looked at Janeen and nodded his head. She took off the Band-Aid from her forehead.

Dr. Giles' mouth dropped open. "It's healed—there's barely

a mark."

"Explain to the rest of us what is going on," Vice President Smith said.

Janeen explained what had happened the day before and how Solomon kissed her and healed her wound.

George stood up to speak. "Mr. Vice President, you think the President is wrong and we should be locked up. You also would prefer that the three million people be taken care of."

"I've never said . . ."

"You don't have to say, you are deathly afraid of us and you shouldn't be. We mean you no harm. Mankind has always been afraid of the unknown and with no reason."

The President stood up. "We accept your proposal. I would ask that you postpone the news interview today so that I can prepare a speech. Allison will videotape you using your abilities today and after we play it tonight, you will take questions. Immediately following the interview, we will take you to a bunker for testing."

"Janeen, you haven't mentioned if you would allow us to test Solomon."

"On the condition that I accompany him and that Colonel Forester join us as well. The patients are familiar with him and I think it would put them more at ease."

"Agreed," the president, said standing. "We will hold the interview here in the auditorium; there is more than enough room for the press corps. I will return tonight at eight for a nine o'clock speech."

President Mitchell shook everyone's hand and had Allison take a picture of him and Vivian.

"You can start waking up the sleepers now. I just ask that we keep military personnel in each of the tents as a precaution."

Chapter 30

Boston Mass, Tuesday, April 17, 2017, 12:00 p.m.

"BEFORE you begin waking people up," Allison announced, "I would like to videotape you first. I think the first thing we should show is telepathy. I've asked Dr. Clarke, Dr. Aster, and Rosemary Stiles, Director of Nursing to volunteer for the telepathic portion of the demonstration."

While Allison setup her equipment, Janeen had the nurses begin to remove the catheters, IV bags, and diapers starting in tent number one.

"Alright we are shooting, but don't worry, I can cut out anything and I won't use everything we tape today. Stephen, how about you start?"

"Rosemary is worried about her husband waking up and what abilities he might have. She wishes they had both gone into the coma together so they could have shared the experience."

"Rosemary, is he accurate?" Allison asked.

"Yes, I am worried that he will find me lacking because I am not like all of you. I know it's silly, we've been married for over thirty years, but it is a fear I have.

"Well, that's certainly an embarrassing thing to say on national television," Rosemary snorted.

"How about you Miranda, can you tell me what Dr. Aster is thinking?"

"He is concerned about all the chaos that is going to go on after everyone wakes up from their comas. He is worried for our safety."

Dr. Aster smiled. "She read my mind alright."

"George, tell me what Dr. Clarke is thinking."

"He is wondering if it would be inappropriate to ask Dr. Corbett to dinner when she returns."

Dr. Clarke turned three shades of red. "Guilty as charged," he said loosening his tie.

"They said you have the power of levitation. Would someone please give me an example?" Allison asked.

Vivian lifted the chair she was sitting in five feet into the air.

Jerry poured himself a glass of water without touching the glass or the pitcher.

As a finale, they stood in a circle holding hands and began to raise themselves in the air and spinning in a circle. One by one, they slowly lowered themselves to the ground.

"Now, I am going to introduce you to Solomon, our first coma patient to wake up. Solomon is a bright little boy with some amazing abilities."

Allison focused the camera on Janeen's forehead. "Yesterday, Janeen had six stitches put in after a rock was thrown through the hospital's front doors. This morning when he awoke, Solomon touched it and it healed."

"I think you should know that Dr. Janeen Corbett is adopting Solomon and they have a close bond."

Janeen put Solomon in his playpen and held up a red block. He lifted the rest into the air and they slowly rotated around. He would say the color of the block and pick it out. When he got to the red and green one, he smiled brightly. "Red," he said picking it up.

Janeen kissed him on the forehead and walked to the other side of the room. "Do you want Jeeen, mama to come over there?" she asked.

Solomon lifted his hand and Janeen slid across the floor towards him. When she got there, he levitated and wrapped his arms around her neck.

Allison focused the camera on Janeen and Solomon hugging. "These amazing people have amazing abilities that they want to share with the world. They didn't ask to be victims of the occurrence, but they want to use these gifts to help mankind. Now, we are going to observe as they begin waking up over six thousand coma patients.

"We're done taping in here, but perhaps I could tape Sam telling us how they are going to wake them up."

"We are all connected because of our abilities. We can enter their minds and simply wake them up. It's much more complicated than that, but it is the only way I know to describe it," Sam said.

"Alright, here is what we are going to do. Allison taped all the information the other day that the coma patients are going to need to adjust to their new world. Dr. Clarke, Dr. Giles, and I will meet them in here, play the videos, and answer any questions they might have. We will wake two hundred patients at a time. Escort them to the auditorium and while they are acclimating to the world, we will start on the next group. Don't expect everyone to react the same way—some maybe jubilant, some frightened, and some confused. We must deal with patients individually and make sure their minds are at ease before moving on to the next patient," said Dr. Hickman.

"We are ready to begin," Janeen announced. "Who wants to go

first? Steve, since you realized you could wake them, why don't you go first?"

"Alright, but I'm waking up Vivian's mom first and she's in tent six."

They all walked to tent six and Steve sat next to Marsha, Vivian's mother, and placed his palms on both sides of her head. His forehead broke out in a sweat and he closed his eyes, deep in concentration. Marsha's eyelashes fluttered and then her eyes suddenly opened.

"Oh no," she cried. "Make it stop."

"It's all over, Marsha. You are awake now. Nothing can harm you here. Look, here is Vivian and she's been waiting for you to wake up."

Vivian ran to the bed and Steve moved aside. They fell into one another's arms and Vivian clung to her mother sobbing.

"Shhh baby, it's ok. It's all over now."

Steve helped Marsha to sit up. After a few minutes, a nursing assistant went to her side to help her stand. They sat her in a wheel chair and took her in the building. Vivian followed, tears flowing down her face.

"It's difficult to wake them up and they do remember the dream so they are going to be frightened, we must convince them it is over."

Without saying a word, Veronica Baker sat on the first bed and placed her hands on the side of a young woman's head. The woman awoke almost instantaneously and began to cry.

"Please don't make me go back there," she begged.

"It's all over and we're going to explain everything to you. This orderly is going to take you to the auditorium where you will meet people who have gone through what you have. Once you are strong enough, you can help us wake the others."

Allison filmed their awakening and tried to hold back the tears.

"How long do you think it will take for patients to be strong enough to help wake people up," she asked Janeen.

"I would say no more than a few hours. Once they realized what has happened they will want to set other people free as quickly as possible. Our first nine patients had no memory of the nightmare; all of these patients do. I do not know if the dream is a warning of what is to come or a mass hysteric dream. I tend to believe it is a warning, one that I hope I don't live to see. Remember what Sam said about their skulls reshaping themselves to accommodate their new brain—that speaks of the growth of a higher intelligence. Though the dreams tell us a lot, they will have to be analyzed and we don't know if they all experienced the same thing."

Janeen's estimation was nearly correct. Within an hour there were an additional seventy-five people waking others up. Some woke up screaming or afraid, and still others had stoic expressions on their faces. One gentleman in particular caught Janeen's attention and she stopped the orderly as he was about to pass her.

"I've seen quite a few different expressions and reactions to waking up, but you seem to have no reaction at all. May I ask why?"

"I saw what was, what is to come, and my role in it all. There is nothing I can do to change the future except to be strong and endure. There is hope for the future, but panicking and hysterics won't solve a thing. We must work together in order to survive. Even those without our abilities can survive if they listen to us."

Janeen followed the man back to the auditorium as Dr. Hickman was addressing a group of patients.

"We will answer any questions that we are capable of answering. There is a lot we don't know, and many of you know more than we do. In the next few months, each of you will be called in for an interview to share your experiences with us. We know that many of you are frightened by the dreams you had and by piecing everyone's dream together, perhaps we will come to an understanding that we don't have now."

Janeen approached Dr. Hickman when he finished speaking. "How do you think it is going?"

"I have positive feedback once we've explained what happened. A few concern me, however. They don't seem as if they were that stable before all of this happened. These are the ones we'll have to keep an eye on. They remind me of the zealots that picketed this place and killed the people in the nursing home. I can sense some deep-seated anger and although this wasn't in the original plan, I'm going to ask the president to hold them for further observation."

"That's reasonable, especially if they're a danger to themselves or others. How many of these individuals are on your list?"

Dr. Hickman rubbed his eyes. "Twenty so far. I want to be present for all the awakenings to monitor this type of personality."

"When I return from wherever I'm going, I would be more than happy to help you," Janeen said.

"I appreciate the offer, Janeen, and I will call you if I need you, but you are going to have a lot on your plate," Dr. Hickman said. "A new job, new house, new baby, one with special needs, and getting the ER back to normal. I do admire what you've done here, though. Dr. Lancaster made an excellent choice when he selected you."

"Thank you for the compliment. But what about you, where does the CDC go from here?"

"We have a lifetime's worth of work to do. We have their abilities to chronicle and we don't know if these abilities will continue to grow or if their offspring will be born with them. We have three million dreams to analyze. Most importantly, we need to find out why and how this happened," Dr. Hickman explained. "But first, we need to wake them all up. From here we will go to each of the Boston hospitals."

"Well, I see you have a new group coming in. I'll talk to you later this evening before I go wherever it is I am going to."

Chapter 31

Boston Mass, Tuesday, April 17, 2017, 7:00 p.m.

JANEEN gathered the original coma test patients together in a conference room and had their diner delivered there.

They, along with the newly awakened, had woken up nearly four thousand sleepers. The hospital had insisted that they all stay at least at least three days to receive a physical, MRI, and an EEG, so the tent cities were going to remain for a while.

Janeen asked if they had met anyone in the Dartmouth area and no one had. She was concerned about her mother and decided to ask Forester later if he could have someone go and wake her up. She had talked earlier on the phone with her father, who was relieved that they had a way to wake those asleep, but she didn't tell him about the horrible dream state they had lived in for the past five days.

Vivian's mother Marsha had declined their dinner invitation and said that Vivian wouldn't be a guinea pig for the government. She had spoken to Dr. Hickman and he had agreed to let Vivian stay with her mother.

The room was quiet while everyone ate and Janeen tried to keep the conversation going while feeding Solomon.

Rosemary had stopped by and taken the time to bake a cake for everyone. Her husband was awake and she glowed with happiness. She brought him with her and introduced him to everyone. He was a quiet man, but obviously madly in love with Rosemary. His eyes never left her face and he constantly found a reason to touch her. Rosemary pulled Janeen aside before she left.

"I know you're going for a week and if I don't see you on the eighth day you can be sure that I am going to raise holy hell. You take care of Solomon and if you can, find a way to sneak into Forester's bed."

Janeen blushed as Rosemary pulled her in for a bear hug.

After Rosemary left, Janeen addressed the group.

"Is someone going to tell the only telepathically challenged woman in the room what is going on?"

"It's the dreams. We're connected to them all, and some are so much worse than what we first saw. We're able to block them out, but for some reason we all need to know what they saw. We've agreed to get together with about a thousand people when we get back to discuss what happened to us. Like a gigantic support group. We're going to rent out a hotel ballroom or something for a whole day. Who knows, maybe all six thousand from today will show up," Steve said.

"We don't remember the dreams," George said. "Perhaps it was because we were woken up so soon. These people have PTSD and who would understand it except other sleepers. They saw the end of this Earth and survival on a planet that is a virtual wasteland."

The phone rang and Janeen picked it up. "Oh my God, NO! Thank you for letting me know before it goes on the news."

"That was Forester," Sam said. "Nathaniel Long's group broke into a hospital and massacred over a hundred people . . . I'm sorry for eavesdropping, Janeen. I'm still trying to learn to control this telepathic ability. Go ahead and tell us everything he said."

"It happened in a small town in Indiana. They dressed in military fatigues and infiltrated a small hospital. They killed all the people who were in a coma with automatic weapons. Some of them were killed by the National Guard. The president has postponed his speech until ten tonight."

"You know," Jerry said. "It's bad enough what happened to us and what we had to go through, but now we'll have to look over our shoulders the rest of our lives. I was watching a televangelist on the TV earlier today and he was also saying we deserved what happened to us because we were chosen by Satan to start the apocalypse."

"I'm a simple man," Joe said. "I drive a truck for a living. I just got married last year and we have a cute two-bedroom bungalow. I never had high expectations of life, I just wanted to be loved and love someone in return. Now that dream is gone and I'm going to have to change my name, sell my house, and go into hiding. That sounds easy, right? Well I can't see three million people being able to do this. It's all fucked up."

"I'm just one person," Janeen replied, her heart troubled by the patients' concerns. "But you have my word of honor that I'm going to make sure the government does everything within its power to help all of you. I have a five-bedroom house, haven't even moved in yet, and you are welcome to come and live with me until you figure this all out."

"I just want to find my mom and dad," Hal said, as he began to cry.

"We'll find your parents, Hal. They aren't here, but they could be at another hospital in the area. The database is up and running and I know they're looking for you."

Solomon slid down from his chair and put his arms around Hal. "Lee," he said.

"Is that where his mommy and daddy are, Solomon?" Janeen

asked.

Solomon nodded his head.

"I'm going to call Lee at McLean's Hospital right now."

Janeen called information and pressed one to have the call connect.

"Yes, this is Dr. Janeen Corbett at Boston Mass calling for Dr. Lee. Yes, I'll hold."

"Lee, yes, I just heard of the atrocity. We've vamped up security here as well. Listen, I have a major favor to ask of you. We have a Hal Christian, age ten years old and I believe his parents are two of your coma patients. Can you look it up for me? Sure, I'll wait."

"Janeen covered the phone and winked at Hal. We're going to find them, sweetie!"

"Just today! That's fabulous news. I'm sending a Guardsman with him right now!"

"You found them, they are okay?"

"Yes, we found them. They were just brought out of their coma today and have been desperately begging everyone to find their son. I'm going to send you over to them right now!"

Janeen called Forester and he said he would have a car ready in five minutes to take Hal to McLean Hospital.

"Would someone watch Solomon while I take Hal out to his ride?"

The group gathered around Hal for a hug. "They found my mom and dad," he said in disbelief, tears rolling down his face.

Janeen walked him to the main entrance, which had been boarded up with plywood to make a security checkpoint, and they walked out to stand on the sidewalk. Five minutes later a young private hoped out of his car and jogged up the stairs.

"Hal Christian, I presume. I'm here to take you to McLean's."

Hal turned to Janeen and wrapped his arms around her. "Thank you, Dr. Corbett, maybe when things calm down I could come and see you and Solomon again."

"We'd like that, Hal. Now hurry up, you don't want to keep your parents waiting."

Janeen had to wipe her nose on the sleeve of her scrubs. She was so happy for Hal and yet deep down she knew she would never know what would happen to him.

Chapter 32

Washington D.C., Tuesday, April 17, 2017, 10:00 p.m.

"MY fellow Americans, today is a day of sorrow and joy. Earlier this evening, twenty religious zealots broke into a tent city and a hundred and twenty-four victims of the coma were murdered. There was then gunfire and a group of the perpetrators of the crime chose to take their own lives. Those not killed in the attack are in Military custody receiving medical attention. I don't have the words to express how grief stricken I am. We will continue martial law and to enforce the six o'clock curfew. Security is being heightened at all the tent cities." His voice changed and the look on his face changed to one of contempt.

"We will charge anyone attempting to harm coma patients with terrorism.

"Now, I do have some good news to announce. Today close to six thousand people awoke from their coma. Although some have experienced disorientation, they are safe and healthy. They will remain at the hospital for three days of testing and then they will return to their homes.

"There has been much speculation about the people awaking from comas and having special abilities. This is true; they woke up different from when they went to sleep. They are the same people they have always been, but their mental abilities have increased. We have prepared a video, just shot today, showing some of the things they can do. Afterwards, we will have a question and answer period with these extraordinary human beings."

The lights in the room darkened. The first shot was of Solomon sitting in his crib levitating his blocks and calling out the color. The next shot were the group levitating in a circle and slowly floating to the ground. There were slides of water poured from a pitcher, which no one held. Then came the telepathy. Allison had left in the part about Dr. Clarke and embarrassed she looked at Forester, who looked as if this didn't make him too happy. The last shot was of Solomon moving her across the floor to give her a big kiss while holding his hands around her neck.

The lights went on and there was loud applause that went on for five minutes. The President finally moved backed to the podium. "I will introduce the people you saw in the video and then you may ask questions."

"Lynn, NBC News—Dr. Corbett, aren't you afraid of the powers Solomon may develop?"

"Not at all; he is just a little boy with a gift. He might have grown up to be a famous baseball player or a concert pianist; instead, he might be able to use his abilities to help humanity in a different way. We all have talents, his are just different."

"Walter, CNN—Sam, don't you feel you're violating people's privacy by listening to their thoughts?"

"I admit it was difficult at first, but it is getting easier to block them out. I don't want to invade anyone's privacy. I've come up with my own technique to rein in my ability."

"Rachael, Fox News Network—Miranda, aren't you afraid that

you might use your abilities to your own advantage, say in the work-place?"

"I imagine there are people that would do something underhanded like that, but I believe in making my own way in the world. I want to be judged on my hard-earned merits, not something I get by nefarious means."

"Mr. President, how are you going to insure that these sleepers, as we're calling them, won't use their powers for wrong instead of good?"

"That is a question I can't answer," President Mitchell said. "There have always been good and evil in the world and there will continue to be so. We will continue to prosecute those who do not live by the laws of our country."

Members of the press continued to shout out questions.

"That's all for this evening," President Mitchell said. He turned and walked away from the podium.

When the sleepers, as the press was calling them now, gathered for photo ops, the President shook hands with each one. "Thank you for allowing us to film and interview you. I'm sure it eased the minds of many Americans. Now I understand you've agreed to go to one of our scientific research sites for our group to test you for a week. We thank you for that as well."

Chapter 33

AFTER an hour-long talk with Dr. Lancaster about what position the hospital was in and about her faith in the staff to finish testing all the sleepers in her absence, plus a tearful goodbye with Rosemary, Janeen, Solomon, and the other sleepers left for the military airport at midnight. Janeen had packed for herself and Solomon and realized she needed to shop for him. There were very few clothes his size at the hospital, and she had only two pairs of jeans and two shirts for herself, so she packed scrubs in the meantime.

Dr. Giles accompanied them along with Jillian Daniels, and Forester. Everyone was exhausted from the long day and most everyone fell asleep once the plane took off, except Solomon who was fascinated with looking out the window. Janeen pointed out stars to him and he grew so excited he went over and pulled Forester's hand to come with him. Forester sat across from her while Solomon went into a long unintelligible conversation and kept repeating the word stars.

"I'm sorry if he woke you up, I can't seem to get him to sleep yet. He's so excited about the flight. His eyes were so wide when we were taking off—just like now, glued to that window."

"For a baby who's been through so much in his short life, he seems well adjusted."

"Maybe because it's normal for him. These abilities don't seem unusual to him and he accepts them. When he healed my head, he didn't even think about it, he just knew his Jeen mama was hurt and he wanted to help her. He is definitely going to be a handful growing up; this natural curiosity about everything could get him into mischief. He surprises me every day with something new and unusual he can do. Take today for example—Hal was crying and Solomon wanted to make him feel better so he told Hal where his parents were."

"You should consider a private school that would cater to his special needs," Forester said.

"I haven't even unpacked yet. He needs a wardrobe, a bedroom, and most importantly, a nanny. He ran around the hospital all week, but I don't think once the sleepers are gone he'll be a welcome visitor, at least not 24/7."

"You're certainly facing many new challenges . . . I brought your bourbon with me—would you like to have a nightcap?" Forester asked.

"I would love to."

While Forester retrieved the bourbon and some glasses from his carry-on, Solomon put his pillow on Janeen's lap and covered himself with his blanket. He leaned up and kissed her on the cheek. "Jeen, mama," he said with a smile and almost instantly fell asleep.

Forester handed her a small glass of bourbon and she swirled it around, sniffed it, and took a sip. It tasted even better than it smelled. "Oh, this is smooth," Janeen said with a satisfied smile.

"I thought you might like it."

"A great way to end a busy day . . . So, I do have a question for you. Is there a chance we won't be coming back from this trip?"

"Absolutely not, you made sure of that. You played it safe and if I were in your position, I would have done the same thing. You've been front-page news and your pictures have been shown all over the world. If you were an unknown, I could honestly say you might not come back, but you should be safe now. Besides, isn't that one of the reasons you asked me to come along?"

Janeen blushed. "Only one, actually—I had other ulterior motives. I like your company and I figured this was the only way I could spend time with you."

"You know, I happen to like intelligent, forward women who know what they want and aren't afraid to go after it."

"My dad says I'm pushy."

"I'll have to debate that with him one of these days."

"So where are we going?"

"A top secret facility in Nevada where medical testing is done. Just one of many, but President Mitchell chose this location."

"I'm not exactly sure how much more testing they can do."

"I know they want to do more MRI image slicing of the brain. More advanced EEGs than the hospital has, CAT scans, more blood work. But I think their biggest curiosity is what abilities the sleepers have and if they are going to develop further."

"I remember there was an old movie when I was a kid and the girl could start fire just by thinking it. Firestarter. I've also seen movies where people can make others do things against their will. I don't see that type of abilities here—I just see a positive step forward in our evolution. It was only a matter of time before our brains advanced enough for many more people to display telepathy and telekinesis. Both have been around as long as humans have."

"What about Solomon's ability to heal?"

"That's not unheard of either. I'm not sure if any of the others have that ability or not. I imagine it's going to take years of testing to determine how these abilities work."

"So true. Off topic, but ex Vice President Pro Tempore Smith thinks that all the millions of people with special abilities should be controlled somehow. Backwards thinking, but if he had a large following it could be a problem. This kind of thinking scares me for Solomon," Janeen said.

"You're correct and from what I understand, Smith and Mitchell are on totally opposite sides. He and the president never got along and I know the president is grateful that Vice President Baker has retaken his office. They woke him from his coma yesterday and he should be back to work within the next week, although he was sworn in again. The president wants to make sure he's strong enough to resume his duties."

"Does Smith carry enough weight to cause trouble?"

"That's an excellent question. He has over half of Congress on his side; the Senate doesn't care much for him, however. He's popular with his own constituents, but I'm not sure they would agree to mass incarceration or any discriminatory treatment—the thought is barbaric. I think Smith with try and back door this by trying to set laws and limits on what the sleepers can do. He doesn't understand the coma patient's new powers and he is afraid of what they might do. He's also a Pentecostal, which have joined in the theory of Nathaniel Long. My guess is that he'll try to keep them out of certain jobs and industries. He'll want them to put them in a national registry, like sex offenders."

Janeen frowned. "That's ridiculous—he can't pick a non-criminal population and discriminate against them."

"Look how it's been done around the world in the past. Hitler and the Jews. Apartheid in South Africa, Native Americans and other indigenous peoples confined to reserves, Japanese Americans during WWII, women, gays, you name it. Our country has a long history of discrimination, as much as any other. Oh, we've become much more civilized, but discrimination does exist and this is a topic that will have the House and Senate debating for months, if not years. What about you, you must have concerns?"

"My concern is for Solomon. I don't want him on anyone's watch list. I'm afraid if it comes to that that he and I will leave the country. I'm also afraid that his power of healing might be abused. It could have been a fluke, because it's me he loves, or it might be something that grows stronger as he grows older. I'm not worried about a career—I can get a job anywhere. To be honest, I don't have to work—I have a trust from my grandfather that I could live on. If I had to, I would just disappear with Solomon."

Janeen bit her lip and looked at her lap. "I imagine telling you this isn't such a good idea."

"You can trust me, Janeen. I would never repeat what you tell me in confidence."

"How about you, Forester, what are your concerns?"

"I have the same fears you do. My biggest fear is loss of liberty for sleepers around the world. Look what happened in North Korea, all those people buried alive. At least our country is more rational."

The PA system crackled to life with news from the pilot that the aircraft was on its descent and would arrive at the facility within a half hour.

"Sorry I kept you up all night talking," Janeen said with a smile.

"No you're not and neither am I. I'm not sure how much contact we'll have this week, but I promise to keep a lookout for you."

Chapter 34

Military Facility, Undisclosed Location,
Wednesday, April 18, 2017, 5:30 a.m.

A truck waited in the middle of the desert as they departed the plane. The exhaustion of the past week showed on everyone's faces. Many were quiet and in deep contemplation, having second thoughts about agreeing to go off the grid. They'd been told they would be here for five days and then returned to Boston, but in the back of their minds, all wondered if this was true.

The driver, a young man wearing military fatigues with no other markings, closed the fine mesh cover over the back of the truck to keep out the sand, and they headed out into the desert. A half hour later, an entrance appeared and the truck entered a tunnel. They continued on for fifteen minutes, and then the driver stopped.

When the group got out of the truck, they stood next to a giant cargo elevator. When the doors opened, it wasn't hard to see that the buttons on the elevator wall read one through fifteen. The driver pressed ten and they began their descent.

Sam's face drained of color and Janeen placed her hand on his arm. "Did I ever tell any of you that I'm claustrophobic?"

"You won't be claustrophobic once we get off the elevator," the driver said. "The facility is spacious and you won't even feel like you're underground."

When the doors opened, Sam was the first one out the door. He leaned over, placed his hands on his knees, and began to take long deep breaths. When he stood up and looked around, he nodded in satisfaction. "This isn't so bad after all. Nothing like I expected it to be."

"Level ten is where all lodging is," the driver said. "I'll take you to your rooms and give you time to shower. I'll be back at 0700 to take you to breakfast."

When he reached Janeen's room, he told her there was a nursery for Solomon.

"No, Solomon stays with me at all times," she said firmly.

The soldier seemed flustered, but Forester piped in. "It was part of the arrangement, soldier. She'll be fine."

Her room wasn't small enough to stimulate claustrophobia, Janeen thought, but it wasn't very large, either, somewhat like a cell in a minimum-security prison, filled with a bed, a small desk with a chair, and a small bathroom with a shower, sink, and toilet.

It didn't take Janeen long to unpack while Solomon lay sound asleep on the bed. She hated to wake him for breakfast and she would have to put him down for an early nap. She pulled him into her lap and began to change his clothes, using a warm washcloth to clean him up. He looked startled at first and then smiled up at her with sleepy eyes.

"Okay, little one, it's time to eat breakfast. I'm sure you're hungry."

She stepped out the door with Solomon in her arms and found her group standing in the hall.

They all looked exhausted and no one was in the mood to talk. A few moments later the soldier returned and asked them to follow him. A few turns through non-descript corridors lined with doors like their own, and they finally reached the mess hall. The smells were delicious, though Janeen wasn't sure if they really were or if she was just so hungry that any food smelled good.

They lined up at a long counter typical of cafeterias. Janeen pushed a tray along and filled a plate for her and Solomon. Oatmeal, which Solomon loved, and some fruit and eggs for herself.

The sleepers plus Janeen and Solomon all sat at the same table and the food seemed to revive everyone. Janeen gave Solomon a slice of orange and he approved, saying, "ummm." She tried the scrambled eggs and he spit them out and wiped his mouth. "No," he said, shaking his head. She tried the oatmeal and he enthusiastically took the spoon away from her to eat it on his own.

They were nearly finished eating when General Harrison entered the room.

"Good morning, I hope you had an uneventful flight," he said jovially.

"General, we didn't expect to see you here," Steve said.

"I wanted to make sure that we got all the testing we needed before we return you to Boston and to be honest, I'm curious about what you can do."

"You've each been assigned a soldier who will escort you through your daily schedule."

He handed them each a packet of papers. "At night, you'll find the next day's schedule on your desk. You'll note there are several different types of brain imaging scans; the second sheet of paper will define what the test is and what it can tell us about your brain. I can pronounce them, but I honestly don't understand how they are used medically. I'm sure the lab technicians performing the tests can answer those questions for you. Along with all the brain scans, we want to see how powerful your telepathic gifts are. A technician will place each of you in a lead-lined room in the facility and we will see if you can still communicate with others. We will also study your telekinesis abilities.

"Now, we are ready to begin. I will allow the soldiers to introduce themselves to you." He waved a group of soldiers forward who had been standing quietly near the mess hall doors.

"Hello, Dr. Corbett, you can call me Daniel. It's a pleasure to meet you and Solomon. His first test for the day is a functional magnetic resonance. (fMRI) We use it to see images of the blood flow in the brain associated with neural activity.

"I know you are a doctor and are familiar with all these tests, but I was instructed by my sergeant to give you a brief overview anyway. This is about a three-hour test. Would you like a bottle or sippy cup to bring something to drink for Solomon?"

"I already have his bottle packed. We're good to go."

"You will not be allowed in the room with him during the testing because of the radiation, but there is an intercom in the control booth. Perhaps you could read him a story."

"Already thought of that too," Janeen said with a smile.

The testing went smoothly and Janeen and Solomon chatted away during the test. She found that he liked the *Three Little Pigs* and had her read it to him a dozen times until he could repeat the story almost word for word.

After the test, they returned to the cafeteria for lunch. Steve sat alone and didn't look happy. "What's wrong?" Janeen asked bluntly.

"I told you I'm claustrophobic and they put me in this little machine to do something called a (PET) scan and a (SPECT) and told me not to move for three hours. I did ask what they were for, but after the third word, the guy totally lost me."

"Let me talk to Forester. Perhaps they can give you a valium to make you less anxious."

Forester walked in and Janeen went to speak to him. When they were done talking, he left the room.

Janeen returned to Steve, who was sharing his lunch with Solomon.

"He's going to talk to the General now or the head medical guy, one of the two. Solomon is having his PET scan this afternoon."

"What do they do it for?" Steve asked.

"Basically, they want to see how your brain is different than a normal brain. The sleepers obviously went through some type of metamorphosis and they are trying to figure out what it is and if it's the same for all of you. There's a really long explanation, but I'll try to simplify it, which is how I used to learn in school. The PET scan shows the blood flow, oxygen, and glucose in the tissues of the working brain. These measurements allow us learn more about how the brain works. It's like a road map of the brain."

"What was the shot for?"

"Radioactive chemicals that show up in the PET scan for activities. Did they ask you to look at images or move your hands in a certain manner?"

"Nope, just had me lay there for three hours, three of the longest hours of my life."

"In the next few days they are going to take images of your brain as if they are slicing it like a turkey to see how each slice works."

"You do realize you just ruined my favorite holiday."

Just then, Forester returned with a small white cup. He handed it to Steve and smiled. "You'll get two of these a day, one in the morning and one in the afternoon. After you take the pill, you won't care what they do to you."

The next three days passed quickly. The medical teams did every possible scan and imaging technique possible. By the fourth day, everyone was tired and irritable.

That morning at breakfast, the General came down and joined them for breakfast. "You will be glad to know that we're done examining your brains. The next two days should be a lot less stressful. Today we are going to work on telepathy."

Chapter 35

Military Facility, Undisclosed Location,
Friday, April 21, 2017, 6:30 a.m.

JANEEN was standing outside of a lead-lined room while George, in a similar room, was trying to figure out what Solomon was thinking.

She turned around to see Forester coming down the hall.

"I need to tell you something, but I need you to keep it quiet until we return home. On a good note, everyone received their contacts to match their natural eye color. The bad news is that I was right about Smith. He's proposed a bill in Congress that all the sleepers have to register. The President went on television this morning saying this was a violation of their civil rights and asked people to call their Senators and Representatives and ask them to veto the bill. So far, it doesn't look like he's going to have enough votes, but you and I both know he'll try this again. It helps that thirty percent of the House were sleepers."

Just then, George came out of the room laughing. "The kid knows *The Three Little Pigs* word by word. I finally had to use my privacy box—that's what I've started calling it—to block him out. He told the story three times."

A technician walked out of a room with an annoyed look on his face. "The test wasn't over, why did you leave?"

George smiled. "The kid told me the story of *The Three Little Pigs* three times—for my own sanity, I thought it best to terminate the test."

Janeen opened the door and Solomon raced to her. He began to giggle. "The Three Little Pigs," he said through his laughter.

"You've got some sense of humor kid," George said, laughing.

"George, we are going to move you to the surface now, and we aren't going to tell you whose mind we want you to read. They'll be in a lead-lined room and we want to know if you can hear their thoughts. If you will, please follow me."

George did a Groucho Marx impersonation that no one seemed to think funny except Solomon, who burst out laughing.

"Dr. Corbett, will you follow me," another technician said as he exited a room. They took the elevator to the bottom floor and Forester joined them.

"We want to see if Solomon can use his healing powers on an animal. We broke a kitten's leg and want him to heal him."

"What the fuck," Janeen said. "You people are sick. This is the last test we are doing while we are here. And we are taking that kitten home with us when we leave."

"Jeeen, mama?" Solomon asked with concern.

They followed the technician into a room and in a small cage was a black kitten with a patch of white over one eye. His pitiful meowing sounded like he was in horrible pain. Solomon walked to the cage and turned around to the technician. Suddenly, the technician flew across the room and slammed into the wall.

"If I were you," Janeen suggested, "I would leave and leave now before he gets even angrier and if he doesn't slam you into the wall again, I will."

Solomon opened the cage and started to cry. "Poor kitty, poor kitty." He touched the kitten's leg and the kitten stopped crying and began to purr.

"My kitty," he said in a forceful voice.

"Yes, he is our kitty now, Solomon. What do you think we should name him? Everyone needs a name," Janeen said.

"Kitty," Solomon said firmly.

"That is a perfect name, we will call him Kitty. Let's take Kitty back to our room with us."

"Bad man hurt kitty. Bad man," Solomon said angrily.

"Yes, he was a bad man, but he is gone now," Janeen reassured him.

"Forester, if I were you, I would tell the General to keep that technician away from Solomon for the remainder of the trip. You can also tell him that he is done testing Solomon."

Janeen picked up the kitten's cage and took Solomon by the hand and they returned to their room.

At dinner, Janeen asked George how his testing went.

"Oh it was very amusing. Jerry decided to sing "Mary had a little lamb" about a dozen times until I told him in no uncertain terms to knock it off."

Jerry began to laugh.

The General entered the cafeteria and made his way towards their table. "We've decided to cut your trip short and you will leave tomorrow morning at 2:30 a.m. Janeen, I apologize for the kitten, I would never have approved such an act of cruelty on a helpless animal. I understand you are taking him with you and with my blessings."

When the General left, Miranda leaned over and whispered in Janeen's ear. "He's lying through his teeth, he was the one that ordered that kitten's leg to be broken," she said with disgust.

Chapter 36

Military Facility, Unknown Location,
Saturday, April 22, 2017, 6:30 a.m.

AS the plane landed in Boston, everyone seemed anxious.

"I hope when I get home that my wife is waiting for me," Joe said nervously shuffling his feet.

"If she's not, call me and I'll help you find her," Forester said.

"I just hope my law partners are sleepers as well; if not, it's going to be a difficult transition. People hate lawyers in the first place; I can't imagine how many would feel about a lawyer with telepathic powers."

"They'll probably love you," Steve joked.

As the group exited the terminal, a cluster of cars waited to take everyone to their destination. Janeen found herself crying as she said her goodbyes. "Here's my cell phone number—I expect you all to use it," she said, wiping her nose with a tissue. They all returned the gesture and after everyone hugged and said their good-byes, they found their rides and left.

Forester stuck his head out the window of the one remaining vehicle, a black SUV with government plates. "Where to, Janeen?"

"It's too long a drive to see my parents tonight, but when I talked to my dad this week, he said that Mom was doing fantastic. Apparently, she's driving him a bit crazy by finishing all the sentences he starts."

Forester laughed. "I think the sleepers will entertain us for many years to come. Do you need a ride home?"

"Yes, I think I'd like to go to my new house. It was a graduation present from my parents. I need furniture and new clothes for Solomon. Oh hell, the list is huge. I asked Dr. Lancaster for a month off to get my business in order and he readily agreed. I'm now Director of the Emergency Room because Dr. Andrews resigned after he awoke from his coma. I guess a few of the employees aren't too happy about that, but they'll adjust."

"Well, it just so happens that I have a week off myself. I'd love to help you prepare Solomon's new room."

When they arrived at the house, Janeen had to reacquaint herself with the rooms—she'd only been there twice before. Janeen let Solomon pick out his own room—the one at the top of the stairs would make a great playroom as well as his bedroom—and then they went grocery shopping and to the pet store to find a bed for the kitten, plus a litter box, food, and toys. Although she wasn't a gourmet chef, she made an excellent pasta primavera, an iceberg salad, Italian bread, and a bottle of Bordeaux.

Solomon fell asleep at the table and Janeen carried him into his room to his makeshift bed. Tomorrow she would go furniture shopping.

Forester helped to wash the dishes and then said he would let her get some sleep. She wrapped her arms around his neck and kissed him. He responded quickly and he held the back of her head as his tongue invaded her mouth. She groaned and took two steps backwards, flushing and breathing heavily. "I would prefer you stay the night," she whispered.

They made love on the living room floor with the fire blazing. He touched her gently and it had been so long since she had sex that she found herself scratching his back and whispering in his ear, "Harder, harder."

Afterward, Janeen lay beside him and ran her fingers down his chest where the droplets of sweat collected and watched his breathing slow as he fell asleep.

Satisfied with the turn of events, she smiled to herself, but found she couldn't sleep so she watched the fire until it smoldered into coals.

In the middle of the night, Solomon suddenly spoke to her in her mind. "Bad man, Mama. Bad man."

She jumped up quickly and went into the foyer. Solomon stood there, holding his lamb. He toddled to her, and pulled on her arm. She followed him into another room and discovered that he was trembling. Janeen's first reaction was that he had a bad dream. To be cautious, she unlocked her pistol from the portable gun safe and loaded it. Janeen picked Solomon up and returned to the foyer and towards the front door.

"Shhhhh, mama. Bad man."

Forester walked into the foyer in his jeans, and shirtless.

"Bad man," Solomon began to cry.

"What's going on?" he asked.

"Why don't you tell me," Janeen said. "How did you do it, mask your thoughts from everyone?"

Instead of looking surprised at the question, Forester merely stared at Solomon. "It took years of practice. Nathaniel Long taught me as we grew up together as kids. He has followers with positions high in the government; hell, if the last candidate for President hadn't lost, all three million sleepers here would already be dead. He predicted this, you know, the sleepers, and what would happen once they all woke up. He said that one would be the antichrist and I think I've found him."

"You think Solomon in the antichrist? You're insane, just another of Long's religious fanatics. So you used me to get close to Solomon."

"Of course he's the antichrist—he has all the signs. He can't be allowed to grow up. He is the one who will destroy the world. You know, at first, I just planned to use you, but then I started to have feelings for you. I figured that once Solomon was gone, we would have our own children and you would forget about him. I just needed to wait until I could be alone with him . . ."

"That's utterly despicable. You. Need. To. Leave. Right. Now." Janeen motioned to the doorway with her firearm.

"So what are you planning to do now?" Forester asked. "I'm a career military man with high commendations. No one will believe you if you shoot me and claim self-defense. After all, I don't even have a weapon. I doubt you know how to use that anyway."

"You're dead wrong about that. My father started teaching me when I was ten years old. I'm a crack shot and I don't miss. Here is what is going to happen. I'm going to kill you and claim I woke up in the middle of the night and you were trying to hurt Solomon. It won't take much digging to connect you to Nathaniel Long. You were right about one thing—nothing will ever be the same now that the sleepers have awoken. You had me fooled. Next time I'll be much more cautious."

Janeen pushed Solomon behind her so that he couldn't see what was going on. "Go back to see the kitty, Solomon. Run."

Forester watched Solomon slowly climb up the stairs and smirked. "You're not a murderer, Janeen; you don't have what it takes." Forester began walking towards her with a menacing look on his face.

"Stop, Forester!"

On those last words, Janeen aimed the gun and shot Forester in the chest. He fell to the floor, his limbs twisted at awkward angles and his eyes opened. She didn't need to check his pulse because she knew he was dead. She dropped the gun and ran to Solomon's room.

"Bad man, mama."

Janeen picked up Solomon and held him close as she patted his back and kissed him on the cheek. "Yes he was, but he's gone now and mama won't let anyone hurt you."

When Janeen called the police, she pretended to be hysterical and when they arrived, she managed to cry, not for Forester, but for the future of the sleepers, for all they would face.

She claimed that she heard a noise in the middle of the night and went to get her gun. Thinking Forester had already left, she was in shock when she discovered him in Solomon's room. He then told her that Solomon must die and his relationship with Nathaniel Long. He tried to convince her that Solomon was the antichrist and that once Solomon was out of the picture, they could be together. Solomon ran to her and she picked him up and ran to the foyer. Forester followed and she waved the gun at him and told him to get out, that's when he attempted to take the gun away from her, and it went off.

It didn't take long for the military to find the connection between Long and Forester. There were no charges brought against her. In fact, President Mitchell called her and offered his condolences, and praised her for all she had accomplished throughout the crisis.

Janeen hired Veronica Baker to be Solomon's full-time nanny. Steve felt like he didn't belong on campus anymore and he moved in as well. She kept the fifth bedroom open for any sleepers who were having trouble adjusting and the room was never empty.

Though Janeen knew the future would be difficult for the sleepers, it might not be too easy for those who hadn't gone into a coma either, judging from the reactions of so many, like Long and Forester. Learning to live side by side with the sleepers wouldn't be an easy adjustment.

Might the world soon belong to the sleepers instead? She had always feared for their safety, but their metamorphosis suggested that the evolution of mankind was in progress.

Other Books By Delena Epstein

D.W. Publishing L.L.C.
e-mail: delenaepstein@delenaepstein.com
website: http://www.delenaepstein.com

Homeless Series:

Homeless

Broken

Judgment

Soul Travelers

Second Chance

Death Shroud

Dream Shadow